Cherish small miracles.

Believe in big miracles.

Above all—hope.

The House
on
Hope Street

Also by Danielle Steel

DANIELLE STEEL

THE HOUSE ON HOPE STREET

A Dell Book

Published by
Dell Publishing
a division of
Random House, Inc.
1540 Broadway
New York, New York 10036

Library of Congress Catalog Card Number: 00-025688
ISBN: 0-440-23700-9

Reprinted by arrangement with Delacorte Press

PRINTED IN THE UNITED STATES OF AMERICA

Published simultaneously in Canada

July 2001

10   9   8   7   6   5   4   3   2   1
OPM

To the beloved friends who
got me through so much,
Victoria, Jo, Kathy, Nancy,
and Charlotte.

To my wonderful children,
Beatrix, Trevor, Todd, Nick,
Samantha, Victoria, Vanessa,
Maxx, and Zara,
who always give me hope
and fill my life with joy.

With all my love and thanks,
d.s.

Chapter 1

It was ten o'clock in the morning on Christmas Eve, when Jack and Liz Sutherland met with Amanda Parker. It was a sunny morning in Marin County, just north of San Francisco. And Amanda looked both terrified and nervous. She was petite, blond, and delicate, and her hands shook almost imperceptibly as she quietly shredded a Kleenex. Jack and Liz had been handling her divorce for the past year, they worked as a team, and had opened their joint family law office eighteen years before, just after they were married.

They liked working together, and had long since developed a comfortable routine. They enjoyed their practice, and were good at it. They complemented each other, although their styles

1

were extremely different. Inadvertently, and more subconsciously than not, Jack and Liz had adopted a kind of good cop/bad cop routine, which worked well for them and for their clients. It was always Jack who took the more aggressive, confrontational role, the lion in the courtroom, fighting for better conditions and bigger settlements, relentlessly backing his opponents into a corner, from which there was no relief for them until they gave him what he wanted for his client. It was Liz who was more thoughtful, gentler, ingenious about the subtleties, holding the clients' hands when needed, and fighting for the rights of their children. And at times the difference in their styles led to fights between them, as it had in Amanda's case. Despite some of the malicious games Amanda's husband had played on her, the threats, the constant verbal and occasional physical abuse, Liz thought what Jack had proposed was too tough on him.

"Are you crazy?" Jack had asked her bluntly before Amanda arrived. "Look at the crap this guy has pulled on her. He has three girlfriends he's supporting now, has cheated on her for ten years, has hidden all his assets from her, doesn't give a damn about his kids, and wants to walk out of the marriage without it costing him a penny. What do you suggest we do? Set up a trust for him, and thank him for his time and trouble?" Jack had his fighting Irish up, and although with her bright red hair and flashing green eyes, Liz seemed to have fiery looks, she was in fact far more moderate than he was. Jack's eyes were dark and ominous as he glared at her, and his hair had been snow white since he was thirty. People who knew them well teased them sometimes and said that they looked like Katharine Hepburn and Spencer Tracy. But despite their occasionally heated arguments, everyone inside the court-room and out knew they were crazy about each other. Theirs was a loving, solid marriage, and they had a family that everyone envied, five chil-dren whom they adored, four of whom had bright red hair like their mother, and the youn-gest boy had dark hair, as Jack's once had been.

"I'm not telling you Phillip Parker doesn't de-serve to get hammered," Liz explained patiently. "I'm trying to tell you he'll take it out on her if we're too heavy-handed with him."

"And I'm telling you he needs that, or he's going to push her around forever. You've got to hit this guy where he'll feel it, starting with his wallet. You can't let him get away with this kind of bullshit, Liz, and you know it."

"You're pulling the rug out from under him, and paralyzing his business." What she was saying

3

was sensible, but Jack's hard-line tactics had worked before for many, many of their clients, and he had achieved settlements for them that few other attorneys could have. His reputation was for not only being tough, but brilliant when it came to getting big money for their clients, and he particularly wanted to achieve that for Amanda. Despite several million dollars Phillip Parker had stashed away, and a booming computer business, he had kept Amanda and their three children living at starvation level. And ever since the separation, she had barely been able to get enough out of him to keep them fed and in shoes. It was even more ridiculous once they figured out what he was spending on his girlfriends, and he had just bought himself a brand-new Porsche. Amanda hadn't even been able to buy a skateboard for her son for Christmas.

"Trust me on this one, Liz. The guy's a bully, and he's going to start squealing like a little pig when we put the squeeze on him in court. I know what I'm doing."

"Jack, he's going to hurt her, if you squeeze him too tight." This particular case frightened Liz, and had ever since Amanda had told them of the psychological torture she'd lived with for ten years, and two memorable beatings. She had left him after each one, but he had wooed her back with promises, emotional blackmail, threats, and gifts. And the one thing Liz knew for sure was that Amanda was deathly afraid of him, and Liz thought with good reason.

"We'll get a restraining order on him if we have to," Jack reassured his wife just before Amanda walked into their office, and he was in the process of describing to her what they were going to do in court that morning. Essentially, they were going to freeze all the assets they were aware of, and cripple his business for the time being, until he gave them the additional financial information they wanted. And one thing all three of them agreed on was that Phillip Parker was not going to like it. Amanda looked terrified as she listened to Jack.

"I'm not sure that we should do that," she said softly, looking to Liz for reassurance. Jack had always scared her a little, and Liz smiled at her encouragingly, even though she wasn't totally convinced that Jack knew what he was doing on this one. As a rule, she had a lot of faith in him, but this time, his heavy-handedness worried her. But no one liked a fight, or a victory, particularly for the underdog, better than Jack Sutherland. And he wanted to win big-time for his client. In his opinion, Amanda deserved it, and Liz didn't disagree with him, only with the way he wanted to accomplish the win for Amanda. Liz felt that, knowing Phillip Parker, it was dangerous to push him too far.

Jack continued to explain his strategy to Amanda for the next half hour, and at eleven that morning they walked into the courtroom for the hearing. Phillip Parker and his attorney were there when they arrived, and he glanced up with a seeming lack of interest at Amanda. But a minute later, when he thought no one was looking, Liz saw a look pass between them which spoke volumes and sent shivers down her spine. Phillip Parker's whole demeanor was designed to remind Amanda who was in control. Just the way he glanced at her was both frightening and demeaning, and then as though to confuse her, he smiled at her warmly. It was all cleverly done, and the clear message he put out to her seemed to vanish in an instant, but not without its desired effect on Amanda. She looked instantly and visibly more nervous, and leaned over to whisper to Liz as they waited in the courtroom for the court to convene.

"He's going to kill me if the judge freezes his business," Amanda said nervously so no one but Liz could hear her.

"Do you mean that literally?" Liz asked in a clear whisper.

"No . . . no . . . I don't think . . . but he's going to go crazy. He's coming to pick the kids up tomorrow, and I don't know what I'll say to him."

"You can't talk to him about this," Liz said firmly. "Can someone else drop the kids off to him?" As Amanda shook her head silently, she looked helpless, and Liz leaned over to say something to her husband. "Go easy," was all she said to him, and he nodded, as he shuffled through some papers, and then glanced up with a small, terse smile first at Liz, and then Amanda. The smile told them both that he knew what he was doing, he was a warrior ready to ride into battle, and he didn't intend to lose to his opponent. And as usual, he didn't.

After hearing the shenanigans that had been pulled by Phillip Parker and his legal team, the judge agreed to freeze his assets and monitor his companies for the next thirty days until he came up with the information his wife's legal team needed to reach a settlement with him. His lawyer argued vehemently against it, protesting hotly to the judge, but the judge refused to hear it, ordered him to sit down, and minutes later, rapped his gavel and called a recess. And within seconds afterwards, after an ominous look at his soon to be ex-wife, Parker stormed out of the courtroom. Jack was beaming from ear to ear as he watched him, and put his files back in his briefcase with a victorious look at his wife.

7

"Nice work," Liz said calmly, but as she glanced at Amanda, she could see that she was panicked. She said not a word to either of them, as she followed her attorneys from the courtroom, and Liz looked at her with compassion. "It's going to be okay, Amanda. Jack's right. This is the only way we could get his attention." Technically and strategically, Liz knew and believed that, but from a human standpoint, she was worried about their client, and wanted to do everything she could to reassure her. "Can you get someone to be with you when he picks up the kids, so you don't have to face him alone?"

"My sister is coming over with her kids in the morning."

"He's a bully, Amanda," Jack said reassuringly. "He's not going to say anything to you as long as there are other people around."

Historically, that had been true. But this time they had really pushed him. She had never agreed to let them do that before, but she'd been in therapy for months, and was trying to get braver about not letting Phillip abuse her, verbally, physically, or now financially. This was a major step for her, and one she hoped that, once she stopped shaking, she'd be proud of. And as much as Jack scared her at times, she trusted him completely, and had followed everything he told her to the letter, even this time. She herself was surprised that the judge had been so sympathetic to her, and as Jack said as they walked back to their offices again, that alone should prove something to her. The judge wanted to help and protect her, by freezing Phillip's assets and forcing him to give her the information they'd asked for months before.

"I know you're right," she said with a sigh, smiling at them both. "It just scares me to get tough with him. I know I have to, but he's a demon when he gets angry."

"So am I," Jack said with a smile, and his wife laughed as they said good-bye to Amanda and wished her a merry Christmas.

"It'll be a much better Christmas next year," Liz promised, and hoped to deliver on it. They wanted to get her the kind of settlement that would allow her to live in peace and comfort with her children. The same kind of comfort, or better, that Phillip's girlfriends were living in, in the condos he'd bought them. He'd even bought one of them a ski chalet in Aspen, while his wife barely had enough money to take their children to the movies. Jack hated guys like that, particularly when the kids had to pay a price for their father's irresponsible behavior. "You still have our home number, don't you?" Liz asked, and Amanda nodded, looking as though she were beginning to relax. At least, for now, the worst was

9

over, and she was impressed by the court's decision. "Call if you need us. If for any reason, he shows up tonight, or calls and threatens you, call 911, and then call me," Liz said, sounding a little overprotective, but it didn't hurt to remind her. Amanda left them gratefully a moment later, and Jack took off his coat and tie and smiled at his wife with pleasure as he unwound.

"I love beating that bastard. He's going to get his when we hit him with the settlement offer, and there isn't going to be a damn thing he can do about it."

"Except scare her to death," Liz reminded Jack with a serious expression.

"At least she'll be scared living on a decent income. If nothing else, her kids deserve that. And by the way, don't you think that 911 business you were telling her is a bit excessive? Come on, Liz, the guy's not a lunatic for chrissake, just an asshole."

"That's my point. He's enough of an asshole to call and threaten her, or show up and try to scare the wits out of her, just enough to make her back down and have us ask the court to cancel the order."

"There's not a chance of that, my love. I won't let her do it. And you're the one who was scaring her with all that nonsense about 911."

"I just wanted to remind her that she's not

alone and she can get help. She's an abused woman, Jack. She's not some clearheaded, tough woman who isn't going to take any crap from her ex-husband. She's a walking victim, and you know it.''

"And you're a bleeding heart, and I love you," he said as he took a step closer and wrapped his arms around her. It was nearly one o'clock by then, and they were closing the office between Christmas and New Year's. And with five children at home, there was no doubt in either of their minds that they would be busy. But Liz was better about leaving the office behind her, when they went home, than Jack was. When she was with her children, they were all she could think of, and Jack loved that about her.

"I love you, Jack Sutherland," she said with a smile as he kissed her. He wasn't usually amorous with her at work, but it was Christmas after all, and they had finished everything they could before the holiday, especially now that Amanda Parker's hearing was behind them.

Liz put her files away, and Jack stuck half a dozen new ones into his briefcase, and half an hour later they left in separate cars, Liz to go home and get ready for Christmas Eve, and Jack to do a few last-minute errands downtown. He always finished his Christmas shopping at the last minute, unlike Liz, who did hers, and theirs for

the kids, in November. She was intensely organized and detail-conscious, which was the only
way she could manage both a large family and a
career. That and the wonderful housekeeper
they'd had for the last fourteen years, Carole,
who was devoted to their children. Liz knew without a moment's doubt that she would have been
lost without her. She was a young Mormon
woman who had come to them at twenty-three,
and loved the Sutherland children almost as
much as Jack and Liz did, particularly Jamie, who
was nine.

As he left, Jack promised to be home at five or
five-thirty. He still had Jamie's new bike to put
together that night, and Liz knew he'd be frantically wrapping gifts for her in the office he kept at
home, at midnight. But Christmas Eve at their
house was everything it should be. They had
come to each other with years of Christmas traditions they cherished, and over the years had managed to blend them into one big warm cozy
celebration, which their children loved.

Liz drove the short distance to their home in
Tiburon, and smiled to herself as she pulled into
the driveway on Hope Street. All three of her
daughters had just returned from shopping with
Carole, and they were getting out of the car with
all their packages. Megan was a willowy fourteen,
at thirteen Annie was stockier but looked just like

her mother, and Rachel was eleven, and looked just like Jack, despite her mother's red hair. The three got on surprisingly well, and were in high spirits as they argued good-humoredly about something with Carole. And all three smiled when they saw their mother walk toward them.

"What have you been up to?" Liz put an arm around Annie and Rachel, and then narrowed her eyes as she looked at Megan. "Is that my favorite black sweater you're wearing again, Meg? Or do I even need to ask? You're bigger than I am and you're going to stretch it."

"It's not my fault you're flat-chested, Mom," Megan said with a guilty grin. They were always "borrowing" clothes from each other and their mother, more often than not without the owner's permission or approval. It was really the only argument the girls had between them, and hardly a serious problem. Liz felt lucky just looking at them, she and Jack had great kids, and they loved being with them.

"Where are the boys?" Liz asked as she followed them in, and noticed that Annie was wearing her mother's favorite shoes. It was hopeless. They seemed destined to share a communal wardrobe, no matter how many things she bought for them.

"Peter's out with Jessica, and Jamie's at a friend's," Carole filled in for her. Jessica was

Peter's latest girlfriend. She lived nearby in Belvedere, and he was there now more often than at his own home. "I have to pick Jamie up in half an hour," Carole explained, "unless you want to do it." Carole had been a pretty blonde at twenty-three, and over the years had widened more than a little, but at thirty-seven, she was still pretty, and she had a warm, affectionate way of handling the children. She was part of the family by now.

"I thought I'd make some cookies this afternoon," Liz said, setting down her bag and taking off her coat. She glanced at the mail sitting on the kitchen table, but there was nothing important. And as she looked up at the view from the kitchen windows, she could see the skyline of San Francisco across the bay. They had a pretty view, and a warm, comfortable home. It was a little tight for them, but they loved it. "Does anyone want to bake with me?" Liz inquired, but she was talking to herself by then. The three girls had already fled to their rooms, more than likely to talk on the phone. The four oldest kids competed constantly for their two phone lines.

Liz was busily rolling out cookie dough and cutting it with Christmas forms, when Carole came back downstairs to go and pick up Jamie half an hour later. Liz still had plenty of work to do, and she suspected that Jamie would want to help. He loved doing things with her in the kitchen. And ten minutes later, when Carole came back with him, he squealed with glee when he saw what she was doing, and grabbed a fingerful of the raw dough and grinned with pleasure as he ate it.

"Can I help?" He was a beautiful child, with thick dark hair and soft brown eyes, and a smile that always melted his mother's heart. He was especially dear to her, as he was to all of them, and he would forever be their baby.

"Sure. Wash your hands first. Where were you?"

"At Timmie's," he said, returning from the sink with wet hands as his mother pointed to the towel so he could dry them.

"How was it?"

"It's not Christmas at his house," he said solemnly, helping her roll out the rest of the dough.

"I know," Liz said with a smile. "They're Jewish."

"They have candles. And they get presents for a whole week. Why can't we be Jewish?"

"Just bad luck for us, I guess. But you do okay with just one night of Christmas." She smiled at her youngest child.

"I asked Santa for a bike," he said, looking hopeful. "I told him Peter said he'd teach me how to ride it."

"I know, sweetheart." She had helped him

write the letter. She had saved all her children's letters to Santa in the back of a drawer, they were wonderful, especially Jamie's. He looked up at her with a warm smile, their eyes met and held for a long moment.

Jamie was a special child, a special gift in her life. He had come more than two months early, and had been damaged first by the birth, and then by the oxygen they gave him. It could have blinded him, but it didn't. Instead, he was learning-delayed, though not acutely, but enough to make him different, and slower than he should have been at his age. He managed well in spite of it, went to a special school, and was responsible, and alert, and loving. But he would never be like his brother and sisters. It was something they had all long since accepted. It had been a shock at first, and an acute agony, especially for her. She felt so responsible at first. She had been working too hard, she had been in three trials back-to-back, and was stressed over it. She'd been so lucky with the others, she'd never had any problem. But right from the first, Jamie had been different. It was a tough pregnancy, and she'd been exhausted and sick from beginning to end, and then suddenly nearly two and a half months early, with no warning, she was in labor, and they hadn't been able to do anything to stop it. He had been born ten minutes after she got to the hospital, it was an easy birth for her, but a disaster for Jamie. At first it had looked as though the disaster might be even greater, and for weeks it looked like he might not survive at all. When they brought him home finally, after six weeks in an incubator, he seemed like a miracle to all of them, and still was. He had a special gift of love, and his own brand of wisdom. He was the kindest and gentlest of all of them, and had a wonderful sense of humor, despite his limitations. They had long since learned to cherish him, and appreciate his abilities, rather than mourn all that he wasn't and would never be. He was such a handsome child that people always noticed him, and then were confused by the simplicity with which he spoke, and the directness. Sometimes, it took them a while to figure out that he was different, and when they did, they were sorry for him, which annoyed his parents and his siblings. Whenever people told her they were sorry, Liz said simply, "Don't be. He's a terrific kid, he has a heart bigger than the world, and everybody loves him." Besides, he was almost always happy, which was a comfort to her.

"You forgot the chocolate chips," Jamie said sensibly, chocolate chip cookies were his favorite, and she always made them for him.

"I thought we'd make plain ones for Christmas, with red and green sprinkles on them. How does that sound to you?"

He thought about it for a fraction of an instant, and then nodded his approval. "That sounds pretty. Can I do the sprinkles?"

"Sure." She handed him the sheet of cookies in the shape of Christmas trees, and the shaker with the red sprinkles, and he went to work on it, until he was satisfied, and she handed him the next sheet. They worked together as a team until they were through, and she put all the trays in the oven. But by then she could see that Jamie was looking worried. "What's up?" It was obvious that he was upset about something. And once he got an idea in his head, it was hard for him to let go of it.

"What if he doesn't bring it?"

"Who?" They spoke to each other in a kind of shorthand, that was familiar to both of them and easy for them.

"Santa," Jamie said, looking sadly at his mother.

"You mean the bike?" He nodded. "Why wouldn't he bring it? You've been a very good boy this year, sweetheart. I'll bet he brings it." She didn't want to spoil the surprise for him, but wanted at the same time to reassure him.

"Maybe he thinks I won't know how to ride it."

"Santa's smarter than that. Of course you can learn to ride it. Besides, you told him Peter would help you."

"You think he believed me?"

"I'm sure of it. Why don't you go play for a while, or see what Carole's doing, and I'll call you when the cookies are done. You can have the first ones." He smiled at the thought, and forgot about Santa again, as he went upstairs to find Carole. He loved having her read to him. He still hadn't learned to read.

Liz went to a closet and took some presents out that she'd hidden there, and put them under the tree, and when the cookies were ready to come out of the oven, she called him. But he was happy with Carole by then and didn't want to come back to the kitchen. She put the cookies on platters and set them out on the kitchen table, and then went upstairs to wrap the set of leatherbound Chaucer she had bought Jack. The other things she'd bought for Jack had been wrapped for weeks, but she had just found these recently, while browsing through a bookstore.

The rest of the afternoon flew by, and Peter came home just before Jack did. Peter looked happy and excited, and gobbled up a handful of the cookies his mother had made, and then asked if he could go back to Jessica's again right after dinner.

"Why doesn't she come here for a change?" Liz asked plaintively. They never saw him anymore, he was either at sports, at school, or at his girlfriend's. Ever since he'd gotten his driver's license, she felt as though he only slept there.

"Her parents won't let her go out tonight. It's Christmas Eve."

"It's Christmas Eve here too," she reminded him, as Jamie wandered back into the kitchen, and helped himself to a cookie, with an adoring look at his older brother. Peter was Jamie's hero.

"It's not Christmas Eve at Timmie's house. He's Jewish," Jamie said matter-of-factly, as Peter rumpled his hair, and ate another handful of cookies. "I made them," Jamie said, pointing at the cookies disappearing into his brother's mouth.

"Delicious," Peter said with his mouth full, and then turned back to his mother. "She can't go out tonight, Mom. Why can't I go there? It's boring here."

"Thank you. You need to stick around to do things here," she said firmly.

"You have to help me leave the cookies and carrots for Santa and the reindeer," Jamie said solemnly. It was something the boys did together every year, and Jamie would have been disappointed not to do it with him, and Peter knew it.

"Can I go out after he goes to bed?" Peter asked, and it was hard to resist him. He was a good kid, and a great student, and it was hard not to reward him for it.

"All right," Liz relented easily, "but you have to come home early."

"By eleven, I promise."

And as they stood in the kitchen, Jack walked in, looking tired but victorious. He had just finished his Christmas shopping, and was convinced he had found the perfect gift for her.

"Hello, everybody, Merry Christmas!" he said, and picked Jamie up right off his feet, and gave him a huge bear hug, while the boy chuckled. "What did you do today, young man? Are you all set for Santa?"

"Mom and I made cookies for him."

"Yum," Jack said, as he grabbed one and ate it, and then walked over to kiss Liz, as a look of mutual appreciation passed between them. "What's for dinner?"

"Ham." Carole had put it in the oven that afternoon, and Liz was going to make everyone's favorite sweet potatoes with marshmallows, and black-eyed peas. And on Christmas Day they always had turkey, and Jack made his "special" stuffing. Liz poured him a glass of wine, and followed him into the living room, with Jamie just behind them. Peter went off to use the phone, to tell Jessica he'd be back after dinner. And they could hear screams as they sat in the living room, when he took the phone out of Megan's hands, and disconnected one of her suitors.

"Take it easy, you two!" Jack shouted up the stairs, and then sat down on the couch next to his wife, to enjoy the spirit of the season. The Christmas tree was lit, and Carole had put on a CD of Christmas carols. Jamie sat down happily next to his mother, and was singing to himself, as she and Jack chatted. And a few minutes later, Jamie went back upstairs to look for Peter or Carole.

"He's worried about the bike," Liz whispered to Jack, and he smiled. They both knew how happy he'd be when he got it. He had wanted one for ages, and they had finally decided he was ready for it. "He's been talking about it all afternoon, he's afraid Santa won't bring one."

"We'll put it together after he falls asleep," Jack whispered, and then leaned over to kiss Liz. "Have I told you lately how beautiful you are, Counselor?"

"Not for a couple of days at least," she grinned at him. In spite of the many years they'd been married, and the children that constantly surrounded them, there was still a fair amount of romance between them. Jack was always good about that, about spiriting her away for romantic evenings, taking her out for nice dinners, and away for the occasional weekend. He even sent her flowers sometimes for no particular reason. It was an art form keeping the romance in their relationship when they worked together, and had ample reason to either disagree or simply get bored with each other. But somehow they never had, and Liz was always grateful for the efforts Jack made in that direction. "I thought about Amanda Parker this afternoon while Jamie and I were making cookies. I hope that jerk doesn't make trouble for her, after the hearing today. I just don't trust him."

"You have to learn to leave your work at the office," he chided her, and then poured himself another glass of wine. He pretended to be better at leaving his work behind than she was.

"Was that your briefcase I saw chock full of work in the hallway, or did I imagine it?" she teased him and he grinned.

"I just carry it around. I don't think about it. It's better that way."

"Yeah, I'll bet." She knew him better than that. They chatted for a while, and then she went in to make dinner. They lingered at the table that night, talking to the kids, and laughing with them. They were talking about silly things that had happened in years past, and Jamie added to

23

the conversation and reminded them all of when Grandma had come for Christmas and insisted they go to midnight mass, and had fallen asleep in church, and all of them got a fit of the giggles because she was snoring. It reminded Liz that she was grateful her mother had gone to her brother's this year. It was hard having her on holidays, she told everyone what to do, and how to do it, and she had her own peculiarities and traditions, and she always gave Liz a hard time about Jamie. She had been horrified when he was born, and called it a tragedy, and still did whenever she had the opportunity, out of Jamie's earshot. She thought he should be sent away to a special school, so the other children didn't have to be "burdened" with him. It made Liz furious each time she said it. Jack just told Liz to ignore her. What her mother thought about it didn't make any difference to them. Jamie was an important part of their family, and nothing in the world would have made them send him away. The other children would have been outraged if Jamie had left them. And it still made Liz angry every time she heard her mother say negative things about him.

Peter helped Jamie put the milk and cookies out for Santa, as he did every year, with a dish of carrots and a bowl of salt for the reindeer, and a note that Jamie dictated to him, reminding Santa about the bike, and urging him to bring some really great stuff for Peter and his sisters. "Thank you, Santa," Jamie dictated finally, and then nodded with satisfaction as Peter reread the letter to him. "Should I tell him it's okay if I don't get the bike?" Jamie asked, looking worried. "I don't want him to feel bad, if he didn't bring it."

"No, I think it's okay like this. Besides, you've been so good, I'll bet he brings it." They all knew he was getting the bike he wanted so badly, and couldn't wait for him to see it on Christmas morning.

Liz tucked Jamie into bed eventually, Megan was on the phone as usual, and Rachel and Annie were giggling in their room trying on each other's clothes. Peter left for Jessica's after he helped Jack set up the bicycle for Jamie. Liz was busy cleaning up in the kitchen and organizing dinner for the next day. Carole had gone to drop something off at a friend's, and Liz had told her she'd clean up after dinner. It was a peaceful, happy evening, filled with the spirit of Christmas, and Liz and Jack were enjoying the prospect of the holiday and a long weekend. They worked hard, and enjoyed the time they spent with their children. They were just walking slowly upstairs hand in hand when Amanda Parker called them. Megan took the call, and Liz went to speak to her, and as soon as she picked up the phone, she could hear that Amanda had been crying. She could hardly talk.

"I'm so sorry to call you on Christmas Eve . . . Phil called a little while ago, and . . ." She began to sob as Liz listened and tried to soothe her.

"What did he say?"

"He says if I don't tell you to unfreeze everything, he's going to kill me, he says he'll never give me ten cents of support, and the kids and I can starve for all he cares."

"That won't happen and you know it. He has to support you. He's just trying to scare you." And he had, very successfully. Liz hated cases like this one, where she had to watch a client she liked being abused. Some of the stories Amanda had told her early on had made her shudder. He had browbeaten and terrorized her, so much so that she had waited years to leave him. And now she was just going to have to tough it out while he threatened her, and they got her the kind of support she deserved to get from him. But Liz knew it wasn't easy for her. Amanda was a perfect victim. "Don't answer your phone again tonight," Liz said quietly. "Lock your doors, stay home with the kids, and if you hear anything suspicious outside, call the police. Okay, Amanda? He's just trying to scare you. Remember, he's a bully. If you hold your ground, he'll back off."

Amanda didn't sound convinced when she answered. "He says he's going to kill me."

"If he threatens you again, we'll get a restraining order next week. And then if he comes near you, we can have him arrested."

"Thank you," she said, sounding slightly relieved, but not enough. "I'm so sorry to bother you on Christmas Eve."

"You're not bothering us. That's what we're here for. Call again if you need to."

"I'm okay. I feel better now. Just talking to you helps me," she said, sounding grateful, and Liz's heart went out to her. It was a hell of a way to spend Christmas.

"I feel so sorry for her," Liz said to Jack when she walked into their bedroom afterwards. She'd been talking to Amanda on the phone in the hallway. "She's just not equipped to deal with that bastard."

"That's why she has us to defend her." He had taken off his shoes and was wandering around their bedroom in stocking feet, silently chortling to himself about the gift he had bought her. But when he glanced at Liz, he saw that she was looking genuinely worried.

"Do you think he'd really dare hurt her at this point?" she asked him. Phillip Parker had hurt his wife a long time before, but they had been separated for quite a while.

"No, I don't. I think he's just trying to intimi-date her. What does he want now? For us to re-verse today's order?" Liz nodded. It was exactly what Jack had expected, and didn't surprise ei-ther of them. "He can sing the blues on that all he wants, we're not reversing anything, and he knows it."

"Poor Amanda. This is so hard for her."

"She just has to tough it out and get through this. We'll do fine for her, and he'll get over it. He has more than enough to give her a decent settlement, and support for her and the kids. He can cut back a little on one of his girlfriends if he has to."

"Maybe that's what he's afraid of." Liz smiled, and looked admiringly at her husband. He was taking his shirt off, and as always, he looked incredibly handsome to her. At forty-four, he still had a strong, athletic-looking body, and in spite of the white hair, he looked years younger than he was.

"What are you smiling at?" he teased her, as he took off his trousers.

"I was thinking about how cute you are. I think you're even better looking and sexier than when we got married."

"You're going blind, my love, but I'm grateful for it. You look pretty good too." At forty-one, no one would have guessed that she had had five children. He walked back across the room and kissed her, and they both put Amanda Parker and her problems out of mind. As much as they liked her and felt sorry for her, she was still part of their work life, and something they needed to forget now, in order to put their work behind them and enjoy Christmas with each other and their kids.

They sat in bed and watched TV for a while, the girls came in to say good night before they went to bed, and Liz heard Peter come in on the stroke of eleven. He was always conscientious about his curfews. And after they watched the news, she and Jack turned off the light and slid into bed, with an arm around each other. She loved cuddling with him, and when he whispered to her, she giggled, and tiptoed across the room to lock the door of their bedroom. You never knew when one of the children would come in, particularly Jamie, who often woke up at night and came in to ask her to help him get a drink of water, and tuck him back into bed. But once the door was locked, the room was theirs, and as Jack slipped off her nightgown and kissed her, she moaned softly as they found each other. It was the perfect way to spend Christmas Eve.

Chapter 2

On Christmas morning, Jamie climbed into bed with them at six-thirty in the morning. Liz had her nightgown back on by then, and they had unlocked the door before they went to sleep. Jack was still sound asleep in his pajama bottoms as Jamie settled in next to Liz. She and Jack had cuddled close to each other all night, and everyone else in the house was still asleep when Jamie asked her if it was time to go downstairs yet.

"Not yet, sweetheart," she whispered to him. "Why don't you sleep with us for a while. It's still nighttime."

"When will it be time to go downstairs?" he whispered softly.

"Not for another couple of hours." She was

hoping to stall him for as long as possible. At least till eight, if she was lucky. The others were old enough not to want to get up at the crack of dawn anymore. But Jamie was overwhelmed with excitement and anticipation. Eventually, she tiptoed back to his room with him, and gave him a kiss and a bucket of Legos to play with. "I'll come and get you when it's time," she promised as he started building something with the Lego blocks, and she went back to cuddle up to Jack for another hour. He was warm and cozy, and she smiled to herself as she tucked herself in right behind him.

It was after eight when Jack finally stirred, and Jamie walked back into their bedroom. He said he'd used up all his Legos. Liz kissed her husband and smiled at him, as he grinned sleepily at her, remembering the pleasures of the night before, and she sent Jamie to wake the others.

"How long have you been up?" Jack asked, casting a lazy arm around her, and pulling her closer.

"Jamie came in at six-thirty. He's been very patient, but I don't think he'll hold out for much longer." Five minutes later, he was back in their bedroom, with the others straggling behind him. The girls looked half asleep, and Peter had an arm around Jamie. He had helped put the bike together for him the night before, and was smiling, thinking of how much Jamie was going to like it.

"Come on, get up, Dad," Peter said with a grin, pulling the covers off his father, as Jack groaned and rolled over, trying to put a pillow over his head, but just watching him do it brought out a spirit of mischief in his daughters, and before he could defend himself, Annie and Rachel jumped on top of him, and Megan tickled him, as Jamie squealed in delighted excitement. Liz got up and put her robe on as she watched them. They were suddenly a tangle of arms and legs, all acting like little kids again, as their father retaliated and tickled them, and pulled Jamie into bed with him. They were one big pretzel of giggling kids and bodies as Liz laughed and finally rescued Jack, and told them all it was time to go downstairs and see what Santa had left them. Jamie was the first off the bed as soon as she said it, and rushed headlong toward the doorway, and the others followed suit, still laughing, as Peter and Jack walked behind them. Jamie was already halfway down the stairs as the others left their parents' bedroom.

He couldn't quite see his presents yet, he had to round a turn in the stairs, but as he did he saw it, bright and shiny and red and beautiful, and as Liz watched his face, she felt tears spring to her eyes. The look on Jamie's face was the magic of Christmas, as he saw the bike, and then dove down the stairs to it, and the others all watched him with pride and pleasure. Liz held the bike for him as he got onto it, and Peter took the handle-bars and led him around the living room, trying not to run over the others' presents. But Jamie was so excited he was barely coherent.

"I got it! I got it! Santa gave me the bike!" he shouted to everyone, as Jack put on a CD of Christmas carols. And suddenly, the whole house seemed filled with the Christmas spirit. The girls settled down to open their presents then too, and Peter eventually convinced Jamie to get off the bike for a while, so they could both open their presents. Jack had opened the set of Chaucer by then, and a cashmere jacket Liz had bought for him at Neiman Marcus. And Liz was thrilled when she opened the gold bracelet Jack had bought her the day before, it was perfect for her, and she loved it, as he hoped she would.

They spent half an hour opening gifts, and exclaiming over what they got, and then Jamie got back on the bike again, and Peter helped him balance it, as Liz went to cook their breakfast. She was going to make them all waffles and sausages and bacon, their standard Christmas breakfast. And as she made the waffles and hummed Christmas carols to herself, Jack wandered into the kitchen to keep her company, and she told him again how much she loved her bracelet.

"I love you, Liz," he said, looking tenderly at her. "Do you ever think about how lucky we are?" He glanced toward the happy sounds coming from the living room as he said it.

"Oh, about a hundred times a day, sometimes more than that." She came over to put her arms around him and kiss him, and he hugged her tight.

"Thank you for everything you do for me. . . . I don't know what I ever did to deserve you, but whatever it is, I'm just glad we have each other." He said it very gently as he held her in his arms.

"Me too," she said, and then hurried back to the stove to turn the sausages and bacon. He made coffee and poured orange juice while she did the waffles and finished the sausages and bacon, and they all sat down to breakfast shortly after, chattering about their gifts, and laughing and teasing each other. Jamie lay the bike down on the kitchen floor next to him. If they'd have let him, he'd have sat on it while he ate breakfast.

"What's everyone going to do today?" Jack asked as he poured himself a second cup of coffee, and the others groaned over how much they'd eaten and how full they were.

"I have to get the turkey started pretty soon," Liz said, glancing at the clock. She'd bought a twenty pounder, and it would take most of the day to cook. And Jack had to make his famous stuffing.

The girls said they wanted to try on their gifts and call their friends. Peter wanted to drop in at Jessica's again, and Jamie made him promise to come back soon so he could help him ride his new bike, and Jack said he was going to drop by the office for a little while.

"On Christmas Day?" Liz looked at him in surprise.

"Just for a few minutes." He told her he had forgotten one of the files he wanted to work on over the weekend.

"Why don't you forget about it till tomorrow? You don't need it today," she chided him. He was beginning to sound like a workaholic. After all, it was Christmas Day.

"I'll feel better if I know it's here, then I can just get up tomorrow and do it," Jack said, looking apologetically at his wife.

"What was that you were telling me about learning to leave my work at the office? Practice what you preach, Counselor."

"I'll be gone five minutes, and then I'll come home and do the stuffing. I'll be back before you know it." He smiled at her, and kissed her after the children left, and then he helped her clear the table.

She stayed in the kitchen to start getting the turkey ready, and half an hour later he came downstairs, in khaki pants and a red sweater, freshly shaved.

"Do you need anything?" he asked before he left, and she shook her head and smiled at him.

"Just you. Unlike some people I know, I'm not planning to work this weekend. On holidays, I take the day off."

She was still wearing her bathrobe, and her red hair looked straight and smooth as it hung below her shoulders, and the big green eyes looked lovingly at him. To him, she didn't look a minute older than when they had married. "I love you, Liz," he said gently, and kissed her, and then he headed out the door with a smile.

He thought about her all the way to the office, and pulled into his usual parking space outside their building. He let himself in with his keys, and left the door open behind him. He unset the alarm, and walked into their office. He knew exactly where the file was, and knew it would take him less than a minute to get it. And he was already on his way back to reset the alarm, when he heard footsteps in the hallway. He knew there was no one else there, and wondered if Liz had followed him, but that didn't make sense, and he

stuck his head out the doorway to see who, if anyone, had come in after he did.

"Hello?" Jack called out, and there was no
answer, but he heard a rustling sound, and then a
strange metallic click, and as he turned a corner,
he found himself suddenly looking straight at
Phillip Parker, Amanda's husband. He had an
ugly look on his face, and he looked disheveled
and dirty and hungover. And then, Jack looked
down and saw that Phillip was holding a gun
aimed at him, and he felt strangely calm as he
spoke to their client's husband. "You don't need
that here, Phil. Put the gun down."

"Don't tell me what to do, you son of a bitch.
You thought you could fuck with me, didn't you?
Thought you could scare me. Well, you don't
scare me, you piss me off. You twisted her around,
got her to do everything you wanted, you think
you're doing her such a big favor, well, you want
to know what you did for her?" Jack saw that he
was crying then, and that Parker had a long
smear of blood on one sleeve, and he looked like
he'd gone crazy. Jack had the feeling that the
man holding the gun had either been drugging
or drinking. He seemed completely irrational,
and hysterical as he rambled. "I told her I'd kill
her if you didn't back off. . . . I'm not going to
let you do that to me . . . you can't freeze everything I own and fuck with me like that. . . . I

told her I'd do it . . . I told her . . . she has no
right . . . you have no right. . . ."

"It's just for a month, Phil, until you give us
the information we asked for. We can undo it anytime. Monday, if you want. Just take it easy."
Jack's voice was deep and calm and soothing, but
his heart was racing.

"No, you take it easy. Don't tell me what to
do. It's too late anyway. It doesn't matter anymore. You ruined everything. You made me do
it."

"Made you do what, Phil?" But Jack knew instinctively, even before Phil Parker said it. Liz had
been right, they had driven him over the edge,
and as Jack watched him, he was suddenly panicked for Amanda. What had Parker done to her,
or the children?

"I killed her," Phil said flatly, and began to
sob as soon as he said it. "It's your fault. I didn't
want to do it. But I had to. She wanted to take
everything I had . . . she wanted all of it, didn't
she? The little tramp . . . you had no right . . .
what was I supposed to do while you froze everything? Starve?" Jack knew it was pointless to answer him, all he could do now was pray that what
Phil said wasn't true.

"How did you know I'd be here, Phil?" Jack
asked calmly.

"I followed you. I've been outside your house all morning."

"Where's Amanda?"

"I told you . . . she's dead. . . ." He wiped his nose on his sleeve and the blood on his jacket smeared across his face as he did it.

"Where are the kids?"

"They're with her. I left them there," he said, crying softly.

"Did you kill them too?" Phil shook his head and pointed the gun at Jack's head.

"I locked them in her bedroom with her." Jack felt his stomach turn over as Phil said it. "And now I have to kill you. It's only fair. This is all your fault. You made her do it. She was a nice girl until you came along. It's all your fault, you bastard."

"I know it is. It's not Amanda's fault, Phil. Now put the gun down and let's talk about it."

"You son of a bitch, don't tell me what to do or I'll kill you too." He went from grief to rage in the fraction of an instant, and his eyes were lasers as they bore through Jack's, and Jack suddenly realized that he meant everything he was saying, and was capable of delivering on it.

"Put the gun down, Phil." Jack's voice was calm and powerful as he slowly took a step toward Phillip Parker. "Put it down, Phil."

"Fuck you, you bastard," he said, but lowered the gun slowly down from his aim at Jack's forehead, and Jack realized that he was slowly winning. Phil was wavering, and in a minute, Jack was going to make a move and take the gun. He never took his eyes from Phil's and continued to advance slowly toward him, and then as he had almost reached him, there was the sound of an explosion in the room, and Jack stared at him in amazement. The gun was aimed at his chest, and for a long moment, Jack felt absolutely nothing, and was sure he had missed him, but the bullet had gone into him so cleanly he barely felt it. He stood where he was and watched, unable to move or raise his arms, as Phil Parker then put the gun in his own mouth, squeezed the trigger, and blew the back of his head off, and as his blood and brains splattered all over the wall behind him, Jack felt a cannonball hit him in the chest, and he dropped to his knees, trying to understand what had happened. It had all happened so quickly. He knew he had to call someone before he lost consciousness, and he could see a phone on the desk as he fell slowly against it. He could just barely reach it, as he grabbed the receiver and pulled it toward him, and dialed 911. He could hear the voice in his ear as he fell toward the floor, but he could barely breathe now.

"Police emergency."

"I've been shot. . . ." He managed to squeeze the words out, and he could see red oozing from his sweater onto the carpet where he was lying.

They repeated his phone number and address back to him, as Jack gasped into the phone and confirmed it and told them the door was open. "Call my wife," he said hoarsely, and could feel his eyes closing as he gave them her number.

"An ambulance is on its way. They'll be there in less than three minutes," the voice said, and he had trouble understanding what they were saying. Why an ambulance? Why were they sending an ambulance? He couldn't remember. All he wanted was Liz. And as he closed his eyes and lay on the floor, he felt cold and wet, and he could hear a siren in the distance. He wondered if it was Liz, and why she was making so much noise. And then suddenly, he could hear voices all around him, and someone was moving him. They put something on his face, and they were tearing at him and pulling him, and the voices were shouting. He couldn't remember why they were there or what had happened. And where was Liz? What had they done with her? He could feel himself sliding into blackness but someone kept calling him, and all he wanted was Liz now, not all these people, shouting at him. Who were they? And where were his wife and children?

Liz had still been in the kitchen in her bathrobe when they called. It was about ten minutes after Jack left, and she had a funny feeling suddenly that it might be Amanda. But she was surprised when it was a strange voice on the phone. The caller said he was a police officer and they had reason to believe that her husband had been injured at their office, and had asked them to call her. An ambulance had already been dispatched to their office.

"My husband?" She wondered if it was a prank. It didn't make any sense. He had only left a few minutes before. "Was he in a car accident on the way over?" But why didn't he call her himself? This was crazy.

"The caller said he had been shot," the officer said gently.

"Shot? Jack? Are you sure?"

"They're not on the scene yet, but the caller asked us to call his wife, and gave us your number. You might want to go right over." As Liz listened to him, she thought about going upstairs to get dressed, and then decided not to. If it was true, and Jack was hurt, she needed to get there in a hurry. She thanked the voice on the phone, and ran to the foot of the stairs to call out to Peter and tell him to keep an eye on Jamie.

"I'll be back in a few minutes," she called up

to him when he acknowledged her, and she didn't wait around to explain it. She just grabbed her car keys off the kitchen counter, and headed out the door in her bathrobe. And as soon as she got in her car, and backed out of the driveway, she found herself praying. . . let him be okay . . . please God . . . let him be okay . . . please. . . . The words on the phone kept ringing in her head . . . the caller said he had been shot . . . *shot* . . . *shot* . . . but how could Jack have been shot? That was crazy. It was Christmas and he had to make the stuffing. All she could think of was the look on his face as he had smiled at her and walked out of the kitchen in his khakis and red sweater . . . the caller had been shot. . . .

She drove into the parking lot outside their office at breakneck speed and saw two squad cars and an ambulance with their lights flashing, and she ran inside as fast as she could to see what had happened. She raced up the stairs saying his name under her breath . . . Jack . . . Jack . . . as though to call out to him . . . to let him know she was coming, and she couldn't see him when she walked in. All she could see was the cluster of police officers and paramedics hovering around him. The paramedics were working on him, and as she looked behind them, she saw the wall of blood where Phil Parker had shot himself, and she felt dizzy the instant she saw it. His body lay below it, covered by a tarp. And then, without thinking, she shoved one of the officers aside, and was suddenly looking down at her husband. He was the color of concrete, and his eyes were closed, as instantly she put a hand over her mouth and gasped, as she dropped to her knees beside him. And then as though he knew she was there, Jack's eyes fluttered open. They had an IV in his arm, and were doing something to the wound in his chest. The sweater they had cut off lay on the bloodstained carpet beside him. There was blood everywhere, all over him and them and the carpet beneath him, and as she leaned over him, it was suddenly all over her too, but he smiled when he saw her.

"What happened?" she asked, too frightened to even absorb what was happening, or understand it.

"Parker," he said in a whisper and closed his eyes again, as they moved him as gently and as swiftly as they could onto a gurney, but his eyes rolled back in his head as they did it, and then he looked at her again and frowned, determined to tell her something. "Love you . . . it's okay, Liz. . . ." He tried to reach out to her with one hand, but he didn't seem to have the strength, and as she ran beside the gurney with them, she could see him lose consciousness, and she was suddenly aware of an overwhelming sense of panic. They couldn't stop the bleeding, and his blood pressure was dropping uncontrollably. Somebody grabbed her roughly by the arm and pulled her into the ambulance, the door slammed, and they careened away from the curb, and both paramedics were working frantically over him, and talking tersely to each other. But he didn't open his eyes again, or speak to her, and she sat on the floor staring at what was happening, unable to believe what she was seeing, or what she was hearing. And then suddenly one of the paramedics was compressing Jack's chest, as blood gushed everywhere. The ambulance seemed to be filled with Jack's blood and she was covered with it, and she could hear the other paramedic saying over and over again . . . no pulse . . . no blood pressure . . . no heartbeat . . . as she stared at them in horror. And as they reached the hospital, they turned and looked at her and the one who had been doing the chest compressions on Jack shook his head with a look of sorrow.

"I'm sorry."

"Do something . . . you have to do something . . . don't stop . . . please don't stop. . . ." She was sobbing. "Please don't. . . ."

"He's gone . . . I'm sorry . . ."

"He's not gone . . . he's not gone. . . ."

45

She sobbed, bending down and clutching Jack to her. Her bathrobe was stained red by then, but she could feel him lifeless in her arms, and the oxygen mask was hissing. And then they pulled her away from him and someone led her into the hospital, sat her down, and wrapped her in a blanket, and there were strange voices all around her. They brought the gurney into the hospital then, and when she looked up, she saw that they had covered him with a blanket, and his face was covered. She wanted to take the blanket off his face so he could breathe, but they rolled him past her. She didn't know where they were taking him, and she couldn't move. She couldn't do anything. She couldn't think. She couldn't speak. There was nothing she could do now, and she didn't know where Jack was.

"Mrs. Sutherland?" A nurse was standing in front of her and spoke to her finally. "I'm very sorry about your husband. Is there someone who can come and get you?"

"I don't know . . . I . . . where is he?"

"We've taken him downstairs." It had an ominous sound to it Liz hated. "Do you know where you'd like him taken?"

"Taken?" Liz looked at her blankly, as though she were speaking in a foreign language.

"You're going to have to make arrangements."

"Arrangements?" All Liz could do was echo her words. She couldn't think or speak like a normal person. What had they done with Jack? And what had happened? He had been shot. Where was he?

"Is there someone you'd like me to call?"

Liz didn't even know what to answer. Who could she call? What was she supposed to do now? How had this happened? He was only going to the office for a few minutes to pick up a file, and he had to make the stuffing. And as she tried to make sense of it, one of the officers approached her.

"We'll take you home whenever you're ready." Liz looked at him blankly, as he and the nurse exchanged a glance. "Will there be someone at home when you get there?"

"My children," Liz said hoarsely, as she tried to stand up, but her legs were shaking and would hardly hold her, as the officer put an arm around her to support her.

"Is there someone else you'd like me to call?"

"I don't know." Who did you call when your husband was shot? Their secretary, Jean? Carole? Her mother in Connecticut? Without thinking, she gave them Jean's and Carole's numbers.

"We'll tell them to meet you at the house." Liz nodded, as another officer went off to make the calls, and the nurse offered her a clean hospital robe to go home with, and helped her out of the robe she was wearing that was bright red with Jack's blood now. Her nightgown was soaked with it too, but she didn't change it. She knew there were friends she could call, but she couldn't think who they were now. She couldn't think of anything except Jack, lying there, and whispering to her that he loved her. She thanked the nurse for the robe and promised to send it back, and then she walked barefoot through the hospital hallway and outside to the police officers waiting for her in the squad car. The nurse at the desk told her to call them when she had made arrangements. Even the word sounded ugly to her.

Liz made no sound as she got in the back of the squad car, and she didn't even know she was crying as tears rolled down her cheeks and she stared through the grille ahead of her at the backs of the two officers driving her home. They opened the car door for her, and helped her out when they got there, and offered to come in with her. But she shook her head, and began to sob as Carole walked down the driveway toward her, and Jean drove in at exactly the same moment. And suddenly both women were holding her, and all three of them were sobbing. It was beyond belief, this hadn't happened to them. It couldn't have. It was too hideous to be true. She was trapped in a nightmare. It wasn't possible that Jack was gone. Things like this just didn't happen to real people.

"He killed Amanda too," Jean said through tears as they stood there holding each other. The officer who'd called her had given her the details. "The kids are all right, or alive at least. They saw him do it. But he didn't hurt them." Phillip Parker had killed Amanda and Jack, and then himself. It was a wave of destruction that had hit them all. The Parker children were orphans. But all Liz could think of now was what she was going to say to her own children, and she knew that the moment they laid eyes on her they would know that something terrible had happened. There was blood in her hair, the blood-soaked nightgown had stained through the cotton bathrobe she'd gotten at the hospital, and she looked like she'd been in an accident herself. She looked like a wild woman as she stood there, staring blankly at the other two women.

"How bad do I look?" Liz asked Carole, as she blew her nose, trying to regain her composure for her children.

"Like Jackie Kennedy in Dallas," Carole said bluntly, and Liz cringed at the image.

She looked down at the gray cotton robe with the bloodstains still spreading on it. "Can you get me a clean robe? I'll wait in the garage . . . and

a comb . . ." She stood sobbing in Jean's arms
as she waited, trying to make sense of it, trying to
get a grip on herself, and thinking of what she
would tell the children. There was nothing she
could tell them but the truth, but she knew that
whatever she said now, and however she said it to
them, would affect them for their entire lifetimes.
It was an awesome burden. And she was still sobbing uncontrollably as Carole returned with the
comb and a clean pink terry cloth bathrobe. She
put it on over the gray cotton one, and combed
her hair without looking.

"How do I look now?" she asked them, she
didn't want to terrify her children before she
even spoke to them.

"Honestly? You look like shit, but you're not
going to scare them by the way you look. Do you
want us to come in with you?" Liz nodded, and
they followed her into the house from the garage,
directly into the kitchen. They could hear the
children in the living room, some of them at
least, and she asked the two women to wait in the
kitchen, until after she told the children. She felt
she owed it to them to be alone with them, but
she had no idea how to do this.

Peter and Jamie were playing on the couch
when she walked in, roughhousing and teasing
and laughing, and Jamie looked up at her before

Peter did, and his whole being seemed to stop when he saw her.

"Where's Daddy?" he asked, as though he knew. But sometimes Jamie saw things the others didn't.

"He's not here," Liz said honestly, fighting to keep control. "Where are the girls?"

"Upstairs," Peter said, with worried eyes. "What's wrong, Mom?"

"Go and get them, sweetheart, will you please?" He was the head of the family now, although he did not yet know it.

Without a word, Peter bounded up the stairs, and a moment later, returned with his sisters. They all looked serious, as though they sensed that their lives were about to change forever, and they stared at their mother sitting on the couch looking dazed and disheveled.

"Come and sit down," she said to them as gently as she could muster, and instinctively, they huddled close to her, and she reached out and touched each one, as tears began to slide down her cheeks despite all her efforts to stop them. She was touching all of their hands as she looked from one to the other, and pulled Jamie close to her.

"I have something terrible to tell you . . . something awful just happened. . . ."

"What happened?" Megan spoke with a ring of panic in her voice, and began to cry before any of the others. "What is it?"

"It's Daddy," Liz said simply. "He was shot by the husband of a client."

"Where is he?" Annie asked, starting to cry, like her sister, and Peter and the others were staring at her in disbelief, as though they couldn't fathom what had happened. But how could they? Liz still couldn't understand it either.

"He's at the hospital," but she didn't want to mislead them, she knew that however terrible, she had to tell them, and deliver the blow that they would never forget. Forevermore, they would each have to live with this moment, and relive it a million times in memory . . . forever. . . . "He's at the hospital, but he died half an hour ago . . . and he loved you all very much. . . ." She clutched each of them close to her, in a bunch, her arms around all of them, pulling them toward her as they screamed in anguish. "I'm so sorry. . . ." Liz said through her own sobs "I'm so sorry. . . ."

"No!" the girls screamed in unison, and Peter was wracked by sobs, as Jamie stared at his mother and stood up, pulling free of her embrace, and backing away from her slowly.

"I don't believe you. That's not true," he said, and then ran up the stairs, as Liz quickly followed. She found him crouched in a corner of his room, curled into a ball, crying, with his arms over his head, as though to shield himself from the blow of her words and the horror of what had happened to them. And with difficulty she picked him up and sat on his bed with him, cradling him as they both cried.

"Your daddy loved you very much, Jamie. . . . I'm so sorry this happened."

"I want him to come back now," Jamie said through his sobs, and Liz continued to rock him.

"So do I." She had never known an agony such as this, and she had no idea how to bring them comfort. There was none.

"Will he?"

"No, baby, he won't. He can't come back. He's gone."

"Forever?" She nodded, unable to say the word herself. She held him for a few minutes more and then set him down gently, and stood up, as she took his hand in her own.

"Let's go back to the others." Jamie nodded, and followed her downstairs, the others were holding each other and crying, and Carole and Jean were with them. It was a room full of tears and sorrow and anguish, and the Christmas tree and opened gifts looked like an offense now. It seemed incredible that two hours earlier they had all opened presents together and had breakfast, and now he was gone. Forever. It was unthinkable, unbearable. Where did one go from here? How did one do this? Liz had no idea what to do now. But inch by inch, piece by piece, bit by bit, she had to do what she was supposed to, and she knew it.

She shepherded them all into the kitchen, and she began to sob again when she saw that his coffee cup was still there, and his napkin. Carole put them away quietly, and poured a glass of water for each of them, and they sat crying together for what seemed like hours, and then finally, she took them all upstairs so Liz and Jean could talk about the arrangements. People had to be called, his parents had to be notified. They lived in Chicago and would want to come out. His brother in Washington. Her mother in Connecticut, her brother in New Jersey. Friends had to be called, the newspaper, the funeral home. She had to decide what she wanted to do. Colleagues and former associates and clients would all have to be called. Jean made rapid notes as they talked. Liz had to decide what kind of service she wanted. Did he want to be cremated or buried? They had never talked about it, and Liz felt sick as they did now. There was so much to think about and do. Hideous details to be coped with. The obituary had to be written, the minister called, the casket

chosen, all of it so grim, so unbelievable, so terrifying.

And as Liz listened to Jean, she felt a wave of
panic wash over her, and she suddenly stared at
the woman who had worked with them for six
years and all she wanted to do was scream. This
couldn't be happening to them. Where was he?
And how was she going to live without him? What
would happen to her and her children?

All she did in the end was bow her head and
sob, as it hit her with full force again, like an
express train. Her husband had been shot and
killed by a lunatic. Jack was gone. And she and
the kids were alone now.

Chapter 3

For the rest of the day, Liz felt as though she were moving under water. People were called. Faces came and went. Flowers arrived. She was aware of a pain so enormous it was physical, and waves of panic washed over her with such force she was sure she would drown in them. The only reality she could relate to now was her constant worry about her children. What would happen to them? How could any of them live through this? The agony on their faces was a mirror of her own. This couldn't be happening to them, but it was, and there was nothing she could do to stop it or make it better for them. Her sense of helplessness was total and overwhelming. She was being driven by a life force so powerful it had no limits, and it felt as though she was being washed toward a brick wall, and could do nothing to stop it. But they had already hit the wall, the morning Phillip Parker shot her husband.

The neighbors brought food, and Jean had called everyone she could think of, including Victoria Waterman, Liz's closest friend in San Francisco. She was an attorney too, though she had given up her practice five years before, to stay home with her three children. She had had triplets through in vitro, after years of trying, and decided she wanted to stay home with them, to enjoy it. Victoria's was the only face Liz could focus on and remember. The others all seemed vague, and she couldn't remember from one hour to the next who had been there, and who she had talked to. Victoria arrived quietly with a small overnight bag. Her husband had agreed to take care of the boys, and she was planning to stay for the duration. And the moment Liz saw her standing in the bedroom doorway, she began to sob, and Victoria sat with her for an hour as she cried, and held her.

There was nothing Victoria could say, no words she could offer her that would make it all right, so she didn't even try. They just sat there, holding each other and crying together. Liz tried to explain what had happened, to sort it out for herself if nothing else, but it didn't make sense,

especially to her, as she went over everything that
had happened that morning. Liz was still wearing
her bloodstained nightgown and hospital robe
when Victoria arrived, and after a while, Victoria
helped her take them off, and gently put her in
the shower. But nothing changed anything, nothing helped, whether she ate or drank or cried or
talked or didn't. The outcome was still the same
no matter how she turned it around in her mind,
no matter how many times she went over what
had happened. It was as though saying it would
make it come out different this time, but it didn't.

All Liz wanted to do was run in and out of her
bedroom to check on her children. Carole was
sitting with Jamie and the girls, Peter had gone to
Jessica's for a while, and Jean was making endless
phone calls. Victoria tried to get Liz to lie down,
but she wouldn't, and that afternoon, Jean said
grimly that Liz had to think about the "arrangements." It was a word she had come to hate, and
never wanted to hear again. It held within its core
all the horror of what had just happened to them.
Arrangements. It meant picking a funeral home,
and a casket, and a suit for him to wear, and the
room where people would come to "view" him,
like an object or a painting, and no longer a person.

Liz had already decided that she wanted the
casket closed, she didn't want anyone to remem-

ber him that way, but only the person he had
been, laughing and talking, and playing with his
kids, and strutting around the courtroom. She
didn't want anyone to see what he had become,
the lifeless form that Phillip Parker had destroyed
with a single bullet. And she knew that somewhere Amanda Parker's family was dealing with
the same horror they were, and her children
would be devastated. They were still young, and
she had already been told that Amanda's sister
would take them. But Liz couldn't think about
them now, only her own. She asked Jean to send
flowers to the funeral home for them the next
day, and she was going to call Amanda's mother
in a few days. But for the moment she was too
distraught herself to do more than cry for them
from the distance.

Jack's brother arrived from Washington that
night, his parents from Chicago, and they went to
the funeral home with Liz the next morning, to
do what they had to do. Jean went with them, and
Victoria came along, and held Liz's hand while
they picked the casket. It was somber and digni-
fied, mahogany, with brass handles and a white
velvet lining. The people at the funeral home
made it sound as though they were picking out a
car for him, and told them of the various alterna-
tives and features, and it was suddenly so horrible
that it made Liz want to laugh hysterically. But as

soon as she did, she was sobbing uncontrollably again. It was like having no control over yourself, and not being able to stop or change the constant wave of emotions that engulfed her. Destiny had put her on the crest of a tidal wave, and there was no way to get safely back onshore. She wondered if she would ever feel safe or normal again, or sane, or be able to laugh or smile, or read a magazine, or do any of the ordinary things people did. Their Christmas tree looked like an accusation, an ugly memory, the ghost of Christmas past, every time she walked by it.

There were a dozen people at their dinner table that night. Victoria, Carole, Jean, Jack's brother James, after whom Jamie had been named, his parents, her own brother, John, whom she had never been close to, Peter's girlfriend, Jessica, a friend from L.A. that Jack had gone to school with, and the children. Other faces came and went, the doorbell rang, flowers and food arrived. It suddenly seemed as though the whole world knew, and Jean was successfully keeping the press at bay. It was the headline in the evening paper, and the kids had watched the story on the news on TV, but Liz had made them turn it off when she saw them watching.

And as they talked about arrangements for the funeral at the dinner table after the kids went back upstairs, the doorbell rang, and Carole answered it. It was Liz's mother, Helen, just arriving from Connecticut, and she started to cry the moment she saw her daughter.

"Oh, my God, Liz . . . you look awful. . . ."

"I know, Mother, I'm sorry . . . I . . ." She didn't know what to say to her, and the relationship they shared had never been overly warm, or comfortable for Liz. It was always easier dealing with her from a distance. Jack had always been the buffer for her when her mother disapproved of what they were doing. Liz had never forgiven her for her lack of support or compassion for her youngest grandson. Her mother thought it had been foolish of them to have a fifth child anyway. Four already seemed too many to her, and five was "ridiculous and excessive," according to Helen.

Carole offered her dinner, but Helen said she'd eaten on the plane, and she sat down at the kitchen table with the others, and let Jean pour her a cup of coffee. "My God, Liz, what are you going to do now?" She dove right to the heart of the matter, without waiting to take her first sip of coffee. The others had all been crawling through the day, inch by inch, and minute by minute, trying to look no further ahead than the next hour, or voice any disturbing questions. But Liz's mother was never one to mince words or hesitate to tread where she shouldn't. "You'll have to give up the house, you know. It'll be too hard for you to handle it on your own . . . and close your practice. You can't do it without him.'' It was just exactly what Liz felt and was afraid of. As usual, her mother had gone straight to the heart of the terror and stuck it right in her face, shoved it down her throat and up her nose, until she could hardly breathe thinking about it. It seemed like an echo of what she'd heard nine years before . . . you're not going to try and keep that baby at home, are you? My God, Liz, having a child like that in the house will destroy the other children. Her mother could always be counted on to voice everyone's greatest terrors. ''The Voice of Doom'' Jack had always called her, but he laughed when he said it. She can't make you do anything you don't want, Jack had reminded her. But where was he now? And what if she was right? . . . What if she did have to give up the house, and close their practice? How was she going to exist without him?

''All we have to do right now is get through Monday,'' Victoria interrupted firmly. They had arranged to have the viewing at the funeral home over the weekend, and the funeral on Monday at Saint Hilary's. ''The rest will take care of itself.'' The funeral on Monday was their goal, the place where Liz had to focus. After that, they would all help her pick up the pieces, just as they were there for her now, and everyone at the table knew she didn't need to worry yet about the big picture. This was bad enough, and as they sat there, Liz's mind kept drifting back to Christmas. It really was a nightmare that would live on for them forever. The children would never again put up a Christmas tree, or hear a Christmas carol, or open a gift without remembering what had happened to their father on Christmas morning, and what it had been like for each of them right after it happened. Liz looked ravaged as she looked around the table at the people who had come together to help her.

"Come on, why don't you come upstairs and lie down," Victoria said quietly. She was a small woman with dark hair and brown eyes, and a firm voice that told you not to argue with her, but her strength was exactly what Liz needed. When she was still practicing, Liz used to tease her about being a terror in the courtroom. Her specialty was personal injury law, and she had won some extraordinary sums for her clients. But thinking that reminded Liz of Jack again, and Amanda, and everything that had happened. Liz was crying again as she walked slowly up the stairs to her bedroom, with Victoria right behind her.

Liz told her to have Peter sleep in Jamie's room, and put her mother in Peter's room. Jack's brother, James, was going to sleep on the couch

63

in Jack's office next to their bedroom, and her own brother in the living room. The house was chock full. Jean was going to sleep in the other twin bed in Carole's room, and Liz had already asked Victoria if she would sleep in her king-size bed with her. They were there like a benevolent army, ready to fight the war on agony with her. And everywhere Liz looked, there seemed to be people. Peter and Jessica were in one of the girls' rooms talking, when she walked past, and Jamie was sitting on Megan's lap. They seemed to be calm, and not crying for once, and Liz let Victoria lead her to her own room. She lay down on the bed, feeling as though she had been beaten with two-by-fours, and stared up at the ceiling.

"What if my mother's right, Vic? What if I have to sell the house and give up our practice?"

"What if China declares war on us, and bombs the house the day of the funeral? Do you want to pack now, or wait until afterwards? If you pack now, your stuff could get pretty wrinkled, but if you wait, your things could get pretty messed up if they drop a bomb on the house. . . . What do you think, Liz, now or later?" She was smiling, and Liz laughed for the first time since that morning. "I think your mother is creating problems you don't need to worry about, now certainly, and probably never. What is she saying to you, that you're a lousy attorney and you can't function without him? Give me a break, Jack used to say you were actually a better lawyer than he was.'' And Victoria believed it. Liz had an extraordinary knowledge of the law, and what she lacked in bravado and panache, she made up for with skill and precision.

"He just said it to be nice," Liz said with tears springing to her eyes again. . . . God, it was so impossible to think he wasn't there. Where was he? She wanted him back, now. Only yesterday morning they had lain in the same bed she was lying on, and they had made love the night before that. Tears poured down her cheeks as she thought of it. She was never going to make love again, never be with him again, never love anyone again. Her life felt like it was over, as much as his.

"You know case law better than any other attorney I know." Victoria tried to drag Liz's mind back to the immediate present. She could almost see all the horrors that Liz was thinking, whether or not she voiced them. "Jack was just showy in the courtroom, like me, we're both bluffers." It was hard to remember not to speak of him as though he were still with them.

"Yeah, and look where it got him. I told him yesterday that Phillip Parker would kill her if we messed with his business and his assets. I just didn't know he'd kill Jack too." She dissolved in tears again as she said it, and Victoria sat down on the bed and held her until the wave had abated, and by then Liz's mother was standing in the bedroom doorway.

"How is she?" Her mother looked directly at Victoria, as though Liz were unconscious and couldn't hear them, and in some ways she was, she felt as though she were having an out-of-body experience, and was watching everything that happened from a place somewhere on the ceiling.

"I'm okay, Mom. I'm fine." It was a dumb thing to say, but what else could she say? It was as though she had to prove to her mother that she could do this. If not, she might prove her mother right and lose her house and her practice.

"You don't look it," her mother said grimly. "Tomorrow, you should wash your hair and put on makeup." Tomorrow, I should die so I don't have to live through this, Liz wanted to say to her, but couldn't. There was no point fighting with her on top of everything else. They had enough to worry about now, without adding family feuds into the bargain. Jack hadn't been close to his brother either, but at least he was there, and it was nice for the children to see him, Jack's parents, and her mother and brother.

She and Victoria lay in bed late that night, talking about him, and what had happened. It was a nightmare none of them would ever forget, and probably never recover from. Liz had already spoken to several people on the phone that day who had told her she'd never get over it, particularly a traumatic death like this, and two others had told her that the best thing she could do was get out in the world again as soon as possible, she might even be married again in six months, who knew, she might get lucky. Lucky? How did they figure that, and where did they get the courage to tell her what to do? Sell the house, move away, move into town, take a new associate in with her, give it up, what to tell the kids, what not to tell the kids, buy a dog, have him cremated, throw the ashes off the bridge, don't let the kids attend his funeral, make sure they see him before the casket was closed, make sure they don't so they don't remember him that way. Everyone had free advice to give, and an endless stream of opinions. She was already exhausted from listening to them. But all it boiled down to in the end was that Jack was gone, and she was on her own now.

She didn't fall asleep until five o'clock that morning, and Victoria lay awake and let her talk all night. And at six o'clock Jamie came in, and climbed into bed with them.

''Where's Daddy?'' he asked, as he lay next to her, and Liz could feel her whole body shudder as he asked her. Was it possible he'd forgotten? Maybe it was so traumatic for him he'd repressed it.

"He died, sweetheart. A bad man shot him."

"I know," he said sensibly, looking up at her as they lay side by side in the bed that his father had slept in only a day before. "I mean now, where is he?" Jamie looked at her as though she were silly for thinking he'd forget, and she smiled sadly at him.

"He's at the funeral home, we're going there today. But he's really up in Heaven with God." At least she hoped that was true and that everything she'd always believed was the way it happened. She hoped that he was happy and at peace, as she'd been told. But in her heart of hearts, she wasn't sure yet. She still wanted him back too much to entirely believe that.

"How can he be in two places?"

"His spirit, everything about him that we know and love, is in Heaven with God, and right here with us, in our hearts. His body is at the funeral home, kind of like he's sleeping." Tears squeezed out of her eyes as she said it, and Jamie nodded, satisfied with her response.

"When will I see him again?"

"When we go to Heaven to be with him. Not till you're very, very old."

"Why did the bad man shoot him?"

"Because he was very angry, and very crazy. He shot someone else too. And he killed himself, he won't come back here to hurt us." She wondered if that was what he was thinking, and she wanted to allay his fears, whether or not he voiced them.

"Did Daddy do something bad to him?" It was a good question.

"Daddy did something that made him very angry, because the man had done some bad things to his wife. Daddy asked the judge to take away some money from him."

"Did he shoot Daddy to get back his money?"

"Sort of."

"Did he shoot the judge too?"

"No. He didn't." Jamie nodded, mulling over what she'd said to him, and then he lay in bed next to her, just holding her close to him, and Victoria got up and went to take a shower. It was going to be a long day for all of them, and she wanted to get ready so she could help Liz in every way she could. It was going to be an unthinkably awful day for Liz and the children.

In the end, it was even worse than Victoria, or Liz, had expected. The entire family went to the funeral home, and they broke into sobs the moment they saw the casket. There were flowers standing next to it, and a spray of flowers on top of it, Liz had asked for white roses for him, and the smell of them was heavy in the room when they entered. And for a long time, there was only the sound of sobs, and finally Victoria and James took the children away, and led Liz's mother away with them, and Liz was left alone with the mahogany casket she had chosen for him, and the man she had loved for nearly twenty years resting inside it.

"How could this happen?" she whispered as she knelt next to him. "What am I going to do without you?" The tears streamed down her cheeks as she knelt on the worn carpet and rested a hand on the smooth wood. It was all so inconceivable, so unbearable, so much more than she had ever thought she could bear, except that now she had to. She had no choice. This was the hand that life had dealt her, and she had to live through it, if only for her children.

Victoria came to get her after a while, they went out to get something to eat, but Liz couldn't eat anything. The children were talking by then, and Peter teased the girls to cheer them up, and kept an eye on his mother as he sat next to Jamie and told him to eat his hamburger. They had all suddenly grown up overnight. It was as though Peter could no longer allow himself the luxury of being a teenager, but had become a man. Even the girls seemed more grown up suddenly, and Jamie less of a baby. They were all doing their best to be strong and be there for their mother and each other.

Carole drove the children home after they ate, and the others went back to the funeral home with Liz. And all afternoon people came to pay their respects, and cry, and comfort Liz, and chat with each other outside the funeral home. It was like an endless cocktail party, with tears, and no food, and Jack in the casket at the end of the room. Liz kept waiting for him to step out of it and tell them all it was a terrible joke and it had never happened. But it had, and it seemed to go on forever.

They went through a second day at the funeral home, and by then Liz was alternately numb and feeling hysterical, but outwardly she was extraordinarily composed, so much so that some people wondered if she was sedated. But she wasn't, she was just on autopilot, and doing what she had to.

Monday dawned with dazzling sunshine, and she went back to the funeral home before the funeral, to be alone with him. She had decided not to see him, and was agonized over it. She felt as though it was something she ought to do, but she knew she just couldn't. She didn't want to remember him that way. She had last seen him in the ambulance, and on their office floor, moments before he died, and that was agony enough to remember without adding further torture to it. More than anything, she was afraid that if she saw him, she couldn't stand it, and would lose her grip completely. She left quietly and drove home, and found the children waiting for her in the living room, with their uncles and their grandparents. Her mother was wearing a black suit, and the girls were wearing navy blue dresses their grandmother had bought them. Peter was wearing his first dark blue suit, that Jack had just gotten him a month before, and Jamie was wearing a blazer and gray flannels. Liz was wearing an old black dress Jack had liked and a black coat that Jean had borrowed for her on Sunday. They looked somber and respectable, and as they filed into the pew at St. Hilary's Church, Liz could hear people cry and blow their noses.

The service was beautiful and brief, the church was full, there were flowers everywhere, and afterwards it was all a blur to her. Jean and Carole had arranged for food at the house, and more than a hundred people came to eat and drink and tell her how sorry they were. And all Liz could think of was leaving him at the cemetery. She had left a single red rose on his casket for him, and then kissed the box, and walked away, holding Jamie's hand with Peter's arm around her. It was a moment of such blinding

pain that she knew that never in her entire lifetime would she forget it.

She moved like a robot throughout the day,
and two hours after everyone left, her brother-in-
law caught a flight to Washington, her brother to
New York, Jack's parents to Chicago. Victoria
went home, but promised to drop by the next
day, with the boys. Jean went home that night too,
and her mother was leaving the next morning.
And then she would be alone with her children,
and have the rest of her life to live through without him.

When the children went to bed that night,
finally, Liz and her mother sat in the living room.
The Christmas tree was still there, drooping as
badly as she felt, and her mother had tears in her
eyes as she patted Liz's hand.

"I'm sorry this happened to you." She had
lost her own husband, Liz's father, ten years before, but he had been seventy-one and sick for a
long time. She had had time to prepare for it,
and her children had been grown and gone. It
had been painful for her too, but nothing like
this was for Liz, and she knew it. "I'm so sorry,"
she whispered, as tears slid down her cheeks and
Liz's once again. There was nothing else to say.
They just sat in the living room and hugged each
other for a long time, and for the first time since

Jamie's birth, Liz remembered that she loved her, and forgave her for the things she had said then. In a terrible way, this agonizing loss had brought them a kind of healing, and if nothing else, Liz was grateful for it.

"Thanks, Mom. Can I make you a cup of tea?" she asked finally, and they went out to the kitchen together. And as they drank tea at the kitchen table, her mother asked her again if she was going to sell the house and Liz smiled. This time it didn't bother her as much. It was just her mother's way of saying she was worried about her and wanted to know if she'd be okay. She had finally figured out that she wanted Liz to reassure her.

"I don't know what I'm going to do, but we'll be fine." They had put aside enough money over the years, and Jack had a healthy insurance policy. And of course she had the law practice to support them. Money wasn't the issue now so much as learning to live without him. "I don't want to make any big changes for the kids."

"Do you think you'll remarry?" It was a silly question, but Liz smiled, thinking of what Victoria had said. "If China declares war on us . . ."

"I don't think so. I can't imagine it, Mom." And then tears filled her eyes again. "I don't know how I'm going to live without him."

"You have to. For the children. They're going to need you more than ever. Maybe you should take some time off from work, close the office for a while." But she couldn't afford to take time off, and she knew it. Their entire caseload was now resting exclusively on her shoulders. Except for Amanda Parker. Just thinking of her made Liz ache for her children and what they had been through that day. They had lost both a mother and a father. She had called the house and spoken to Amanda's sister that afternoon and told her how sorry she was. They had both cried, and the Parker family had sent her and the children flowers.

"I can't close the office, Mom. I have a responsibility to our clients."

"That's too much burden for you, Liz." Her mother cried as she said it. She had a heart after all. It was just the connection to her mouth that was so often foolish and faulty, but Liz suddenly understood something more about her. She meant well, she just didn't know how to say it.

"I'll manage."

"Do you want me to stay?"

Liz shook her head. She'd just have to take care of her mother if she stayed, and she needed all her energy now for her children. "I'll call if I need you. I promise." The two women held hands across the kitchen table, and then went up to bed. Victoria called her late that night to see how she was, and she said she was fine, but neither of them believed it, and Liz lay in bed, wide awake, and crying most of the night, until six o'clock the next morning.

Her mother left on schedule, and then she and the children were alone, roaming aimlessly around the house. Carole took everyone bowling that afternoon, and even Peter went, for once without his girlfriend. Liz stayed home to go through some of Jack's papers, and everything was meticulously organized. She found his will easily, the insurance policy, everything was in order in his desk. There was no chaos to comb through, no bad surprises, nothing to worry her, except for the fact that he was gone and she was alone for the rest of her life. And as she thought of it, she felt the now familiar wave of panic wash over her, and she missed him more than she thought humanly possible. She cried all afternoon, and by the time the kids came home, she looked exhausted.

Carole cooked dinner for them that night, hamburgers and french fries. They had thrown the turkey out, untouched, on Christmas night. No one wanted to look at it, let alone eat it. And by nine o'clock, the children were in their rooms, the girls watched a video, and later that night, Jamie woke up and climbed into bed with her, and it was comforting to have him there, warm and cozy beside her. Life stretched ahead of her like an endless empty strip of road now, with nothing but responsibilities and burdens, and things she would have to do alone.

The next week crawled by, the kids were still home from school for the Christmas holiday. On Sunday they went to church. He had been gone for ten days by then. Ten days. Days, only hours and moments. It still felt like a nightmare. And on Monday morning, she got up and cooked them breakfast. Peter drove himself to school, and she took the girls to their school nearby, and then drove Jamie to his special school, but he hesitated for a long time before he got out of the car. And at last, he turned and looked up at his mother, as he clutched his lunch box. It was a new one that Rachel had given him for Christmas with *Star Wars* figures on it.

"Do I have to tell them at school that Daddy died?" he asked, looking somber.

"The teachers know. I called to tell them, and I think everybody read it in the newspaper, sweetheart. Just say you don't want to talk about it, if you don't want to."

"Do they know a bad man shot him?"

"I think so." She had told the woman who ran the school that if he got upset and wanted to come home, they should call Carole, or Liz herself at the office. But like the other children, he seemed to be doing better than she'd expected. "If you need to call me at the office to talk to me, just tell your teacher, she'll let you."

"Can I come home if I want to?" He looked worried.

"Sure. But you might get pretty lonely. It might be more fun at school, with your friends. See how you feel after a while." He nodded then, and opened the car door, hesitated for an instant and then turned to look back at her.

"What if someone shoots you at the office, Mom?" His eyes were full of tears as he asked her, and she shook her head with tears in her own eyes.

"That won't happen, I promise." She reached out and touched him gently as she said it. But how could she promise him that? How could she promise him that any of them would ever be safe again? How could she know? If something so terrible could happen to Jack, terrible things could happen to any of them, and now they all knew it, even Jamie. There were no guarantees anymore for long life or safety. "I'm going to be fine. And so will you. I'll see you tonight, sweetheart." He nodded and got out of the car, and walked forlornly into school as she watched him with a bowling ball on her heart. She couldn't help wondering if they would all feel like this forever, or for a very long time at least. It was hard to imagine feeling good again, or laughing, or making noise, or being loud, or feeling their hearts light. This seemed like a burden they would carry with them forever, or at least she knew she would. They would get over it, or at least adjust to it. But they would never have another father, and she would never have Jack. Their loss was irreparable, even if their hearts repaired eventually, there would always be a hole there. And as she drove to the office, she was so blinded by tears and so worried about all of them, that she drove through two red lights and got pulled over by a policeman.

"Did you see that light?" he barked at her as she rolled the window down, and she apologized through her tears. He looked at her long and hard as he took her driver's license from her, started to walk away and then turned back. He had recognized the name, and had read about it in the papers. He looked at her with concern, as he gave her back her license. "You shouldn't be driving. Where are you going?"

"To work." He nodded and met her eyes.

"I'm sorry about your husband. Why don't you follow me? What's the address?" She gave it to him, and he got back in his car, turned on the flashing lights and pulled ahead of her, and escorted her all the way to their office, as she cried.

It was almost worse when people were nice. But he had been incredibly decent to her. He got out as she parked the car, and then shook her hand. "Try not to drive for a while, or as little as possible. You could get in an accident, hurt someone, or yourself. Give it a little time." He patted her arm, and she was still crying when she thanked him, and walked into her office, carrying Jack's briefcase.

She hadn't been at the office since Jack died, and she was dreading the sight of it, but she knew Jean had been busy the week before. As usual, she had worked miracles. The bloodstained carpet had been replaced, the wall where Phillip Parker had shot himself had been repainted. There was no sign of the carnage that had taken place, and Jean smiled up at her as she walked in, and offered her a cup of coffee.

"Was that a black and white I saw outside a minute ago?" Jean looked concerned, as Liz blew her nose and smiled at her. She wanted to thank her for all she'd done to clean things up, but she just couldn't bring herself to say it. Jean understood without hearing the words, and handed her a steaming mug of black coffee.

"I ran two red lights on the way here. He was very nice, and gave me an escort right to the door. He told me to stay off the roads."

"Not a bad idea," Jean said, looking worried.

"What do you suggest I do? Hire a limo? I've got to come to work."

"Take a cab," Jean said sensibly.

"That's silly."

"Not as silly as killing yourself or someone else. Now, *that's* silly."

"I'm okay," Liz reassured her, but convinced no one.

Jean had cancelled all the court appearances she could, save two which couldn't be postponed, but they weren't until later that week. Liz needed the time to go through all their files, and figure out what she was going to do about their clients. She dictated a letter to Jean that afternoon, explaining the circumstances of Jack's death to all their active clients, although it was hard to believe anyone didn't know. It had been all over the news during the Christmas weekend. But some might have been away, or missed it somehow. She explained that she'd be working as a sole practitioner now, and understood if people wanted to hire other attorneys to replace them. If not, she would be continuing with their work, and doing the best possible job for them. And to those who had sent her letters and flowers, she thanked them for their expressions of sympathy. The letter was direct and to the point, and both she and Jean suspected that most of their clients would stick with her. But that vote of confidence in itself was going to be an enormous burden to her. Despite what she had said to her mother the week before, she was beginning to wonder if she could do it. It was going to be hell doing it all alone. Overnight, it had more than doubled her workload. Not only did she have to handle his work as well as her own, but she had lost the moral support and the spark and the energy that he brought to her.

"Think I can do it?" she asked Jean at the end of the afternoon, looking depressed and anxious. Everything seemed to take ten times as much effort, and she felt exhausted.

"Of course you can." Jean knew that Liz was every bit as good an attorney as Jack was. He had been the bluster and the balls and the bully in the partnership, if he had to be. But they had done a skillful dance together.

But at that moment, without him, Liz felt like less than half the team. She felt as though he had taken her confidence and her courage with him, and said so to Jean. "You'll be fine," Jean said again. "And I'll do everything I can to help you."

"I know you will, Jean. You already have." She glanced at the brand-new carpeting and back at her secretary, as her eyes filled with tears and she remembered all too painfully how it had looked on Christmas morning. "Thank you," she whispered, and went to sit in her husband's office. She was still going through his files, and she had to force herself to leave at five-thirty. She didn't want to come home too late for the kids, although she knew she could have stayed at the office till midnight every night for a month, and still not finished everything she wanted. She took his briefcase home with her, chock-full of files she wanted to read before morning. And she still had the two court appearances to prepare for.

The house was silent when she got in, unusually so, she actually wondered if anyone was home, and then she saw Jamie sitting quietly with Carole in the kitchen. She had just made chocolate chip cookies for him, and he was at the kitchen table, eating one in total silence. He said not a word to anyone, not even to his mother as she walked in and smiled at him.

"How was your day, sweetheart?"

"Sad," he said honestly. "My teacher cried when she said she was sorry about Daddy." Liz nodded. She knew only too well now what that felt like. The delivery boy who brought her sandwich to the office for lunch had made her cry, as had the pharmacist when she stopped to refill a prescription, as had two people she'd run into on the street, as did everyone now. All they had to do was say they were sorry, and it nearly killed her. If they had kicked her in the shins, it would have been easier to deal with. And the avalanche of condolence letters that had come to the office

Danielle Steel

broke her heart as she read them. And when she glanced at the kitchen counter, she saw another stack there. People meant well, but their eloquence and their expressions of sympathy were agony to live with.

"How's everyone else?" Liz asked Carole as she set down Jack's briefcase.

"Why are you carrying Daddy's bag?" Jamie asked, as he ate another cookie.

"I need to read some of his papers." Jamie nodded, satisfied, and informed her that Rachel had been crying in her room, but Annie and Megan were on the phone, and Peter hadn't come home yet.

"He said he'd teach me how to ride my new bike, but he hasn't," Jamie said sadly. The bike had been all but forgotten.

"Maybe he can do it tonight," she said hopefully, but Jamie shook his head and put down a half-eaten cookie. Like her, and the others, he had no appetite.

"I don't want to ride my bike now."

"Okay," she said softly, as she touched his silky hair and bent down to kiss him, as Peter walked in the kitchen door with a ravaged expression. "Hi, Peter." She didn't dare ask him how his day was, she could see it. The same way all of theirs had been. He looked as though he'd aged five years in the past week. It was a familiar feeling. But she felt a hundred years older than she had on Christmas Eve. She had barely eaten or slept in the past week, and she looked it.

"I've got something to tell you, Mom."

"Why is it that I don't get the feeling it's good news?" she said with a sigh, as she sat down and picked up the rest of Jamie's cookie. Her lunch had sat untouched all afternoon in her office.

"I had an accident on the way home from school."

"Did you hurt anyone?" She looked calm, but she was numb, and her perspective had changed in the last week. Anything less than death was something she could live with.

"Just the car. I hit a parked car, and crumpled the front fender."

"Did you leave a note for the owner of the other car?" He nodded in answer.

"It didn't do anything to them, but I left a note anyway. I'm sorry, Mom."

"It's okay, sweetheart. I ran two red lights on the way to work this morning, if that makes you feel any better. The officer who stopped me said I shouldn't be driving. Maybe you shouldn't either, for a while."

"I can't get anywhere if I don't, Mom."

"I know, neither can I. We'll just both have to be careful." He drove an old Volvo station wagon that Jack had bought for him that year because it was safe and solid, and she was glad for it now. She drove a newer model of the same car, and Carole had her own car, an old Ford that she'd had for ten years and kept in mint condition. It got her where she wanted to go, and she picked the children up from school in it. There was Jack's car now too, a new Lexus he had splurged on that year, but Liz didn't have the heart to drive it herself or sell it. Maybe they'd just keep it. She couldn't bear the thought of disposing of his things. She'd already spent several nights holding his clothes close to her, and smelling the familiar aftershave on them, as she stood in his closet. She couldn't bear to part with any of his belongings, and had no intention of giving away anything. She still needed to keep his things near her. Several people had told her to get rid of everything as soon as possible, and she had thanked them for their concern, and had every intention of ignoring what they told her.

The girls came downstairs for dinner shortly after that, and they were a somber group as they sat at the kitchen table. And for at least half the meal, no one said a word. They looked and felt like survivors of the *Titanic.* Just getting through the days now was gruelling, particularly now that they were back at school and she was back in the office.

"Do I dare ask how everyone's first day back

at school was?'' she finally asked them, as she looked at the uneaten food on everyone's plates. Only Peter had made a vague effort to eat anything, and even he wasn't up to his usual standards. He usually had seconds of everything, and ice cream on whatever was served for dessert, regardless of what it was. But no one could eat, and they looked relieved when their mother asked them how their day was.

"It sucked," Rachel volunteered first, and Annie seconded the opinion.

"Everyone kept asking how it happened, if I saw him afterwards, if we cried at the funeral. It was sick," Megan said, as the others heaved a sigh of agreement.

"They mean well, probably," Liz gave them the benefit of the doubt, "they're just curious and they don't know what to say to us. We just have to keep trucking and get through it."

"I don't want to go back to school," Jamie said firmly, and Liz was about to tell him he had to, when she decided he didn't. If he needed some time at home to heal, what difference did it make, particularly for Jamie.

"Maybe you can keep Carole company for a few days," Liz said quietly, and Rachel immediately looked at her with a question.

"Can I stay home too?"

"Can I?" Annie echoed.

"I think you guys need to try and work through it. Maybe Jamie can give it another try next week." Peter didn't tell anyone at the table he had cut his last two classes and sat in the gym alone, but he just couldn't face more of what his sisters had been describing. The coach had found him there, and they had talked for a long time. He had lost his father when he was the same age as Peter, and they had talked about what it felt like. It helped to hear his coach but it couldn't take away the pain.

"No one said this was going to be easy," Liz said with a sigh. "But this is what life dished out to us for right now. We have to try and make the best of it. Maybe if we just do it for Daddy, he would have wanted us to be okay. And one day, we will be again."

"When?" Annie asked miserably. "How long will we feel like this? The rest of our lives?"

"It feels like that right now. I don't know," Liz said honestly. "How long does anything hurt? A long time sometimes, but not forever." She wished she believed that herself as they all went back upstairs again. The house had never been as quiet. They were all in their rooms with their doors closed, there was no sound of music blaring from within, and the phone hardly rang. Liz kissed them all good night when they went to bed, even Peter, and they hugged each other for a long time without words. There was nothing left to say. All they could do now was survive it. And Jamie slept in her bed again that night. She didn't encourage him to go back to his own bed, because it was so nice having him there so she didn't have to sleep alone. But all she could think of as she turned off the light and lay next to her sleeping child was how much she missed Jack, and ask herself, and him, if he could see her from where he was, how she was ever going to get through this. There were no answers yet. There was no joy left in their life. Only the unbearable agony of losing him, and the gaping hole he had left, which was only filled with the pain of missing him. It was still a physical ache for all of them, and especially for her, as she lay awake again all night, crying for him, and holding on to Jamie. She felt as though she were drowning as she clung to her youngest child.

Chapter 4

By Valentine's Day, Jack had been gone for seven weeks, and the kids were starting to feel better. Liz had talked to the girls' school psychologist, who had given her the mixed blessing of telling her that somewhere around six to eight weeks, the kids would turn the corner, and start to be happier again. They would adjust, but by then, Liz would feel worse for a while, as the full reality of it hit her.

And as she walked into the office on Valentine's Day, Liz finally believed her. Jack had always made a big deal out of holidays. He bought roses for her on Valentine's Day, and he always got her a present. But everything about this year was different. She had to appear in court for clients twice that day, and she was finding it harder and harder to do that. Her clients' animosity toward the spouses they were divorcing seemed unnecessarily venomous to her, and the cruel tricks they pulled on each other and wanted her to pull on their behalf seemed so pointless. She was beginning to hate their law practice, and wondered why she had let Jack talk her into family law in the first place.

She had said as much to Victoria when she last talked to her. Her boys kept her busy as they were still in nursery school, and she and Liz had had trouble getting together, but they still had time for long conversations on the phone late at night.

"What other kind of law would you rather do?" Victoria had asked sensibly. "You always told me you hated personal injury when I was doing it, and I can't see you doing criminal."

"There are other specialties. I don't know, maybe something to do with kids. All my clients are so busy trying to screw each other over, they forget about their children." Children's advocacy had always appealed to her, but Jack had always been quick to remind her there was no money in it. He wasn't greedy, but he was practical, and they had five kids to support. They made a good living in family law, and it was difficult to ignore that.

But she was reminded again of how much she hated it on the afternoon of Valentine's Day when she walked out of court having won some minor point for one of her clients. She had allowed herself to get talked into filing a motion against the woman's ex-husband more for its nuisance value than for any real legal reason, and the judge had correctly scolded her for it, but granted the motion. The victory was hollow for her as a result, and she felt stupid as she drove back to the office.

"Did you lose?" Jean asked when she saw her walk into the office. Liz looked tired and annoyed and seemed irritable when she picked up her messages on the way into her office.

"No. We won. But the judge said it was frivolous, and he was right. I don't know why I let her talk me into it. All she really wanted to do was annoy him. Jack would have put his foot down." But Jack wasn't there anymore to discuss things with, or bounce things off of, or make her laugh, and keep their clients in line. He had made it fun for her, and kept their practice exciting. Now it was just drudgery, and she no longer felt she was doing the best possible job for their clients. "Maybe my mother was right two months ago, and I should close the office."

"I don't think so," Jean said quietly, "unless that's what you want to do." She knew the insurance money had come in the week before, and Liz could afford to close the office for a while and decide what she wanted to do, but she thought she'd be miserable sitting at home with too much time on her hands. She had worked for too long, done it too well, and had enjoyed it too much to just give it up now. "Give it time, maybe it'll get to be fun again for you, Liz. Or maybe you just have to put your foot down with your clients, and be more selective about the cases you take now."

"Yeah. Maybe." She left early that afternoon, and didn't tell anyone where she was going. There was something she wanted to do, and she knew she had to do it alone. She stopped and bought a dozen roses on the way out of town, and she drove to the cemetery, and stood at his grave for a long time. There was no headstone yet, and she laid the roses down on the grass, and then stood there and cried for an hour, racked by sobs.

"I love you," she whispered finally, and then walked away in the chill wind, with her head down, and her hands deep in her pockets. She cried all the way home, and she was just a few blocks away when she missed a stop sign, and rolled blindly through it, just as a young woman left the curb and dashed across the street. Liz's Volvo and the young woman's left hip collided instantly, and she crumpled toward the ground with a startled expression as Liz stomped on the brakes, put the car into park, and leapt out of the car to help her. There were still tears on her face as she helped the young woman up, and three cars honked at her, and people shouted out their windows at her.

"What are you? Crazy, or drunk? I saw that!"

"You hit her! I was a witness. . . . You okay?" the driver shouted to her victim, as both women stood trembling in front of Liz's car, and tears continued to pour down Liz's face.

"I'm so sorry, I . . . I don't know what happened. I didn't see the stop sign," she said to her victim, but she did know what had happened. She had been to the cemetery to see Jack and she was so distraught she had hit the woman who had every right to be crossing the street. It was entirely Liz's fault, and she herself knew it.

"I'm okay . . . don't worry. . . . You just barely touched me," the young woman reassured her.

"I could have killed you," Liz said in horror, and both women were holding each other's arms, as though to hold each other up, and the woman who'd been hit looked at Liz, and realized Liz was in a daze.

"Are you okay?" Liz nodded in answer, barely able to speak, desperately sorry about what had happened, and frightened of what could have.

"I'm so sorry . . . my husband just died . . . and I was at the cemetery just now . . . I shouldn't have been driving. . . ."

"Why don't we both sit down. . . ." They both got into Liz's car, and she offered to take the woman to the hospital, but the young woman insisted she was fine, and told Liz she was sorry about her husband. Liz was in far worse shape than she was.

"Are you sure you don't want to go to a doctor?" Liz asked her again, but the young woman smiled, grateful that nothing worse had happened.

"I'm fine. The worst I'll get is a bruise. We were both lucky . . . or at least, I was." They sat there together for a little while, exchanged names and telephone numbers, and a few minutes later the young woman got up and went on her way, and Liz went home, still shaking. She called Victoria from her car and told her what had happened, since personal injury had been her specialty. Victoria whistled through her teeth when Liz told her.

"If she's as nice as you say, which I doubt, from experience, you were goddamn lucky. You'd better give up driving for a while, Liz, before you kill somebody."

"I've been okay . . . it was just today. . . . I

went out to the cemetery . . . it's Valentine's Day. . . .'' She started to sob and couldn't say more.

"I know. I'm so sorry. I know how hard this is." But she didn't. No one could possibly know, Liz knew now, unless they'd been through it. She realized that all the times she had told people who had lost someone how sorry she was, she hadn't been able to dream, for a single instant, of what it meant to them, or what it felt like.

She told the children about the accident that night, and they looked frightened, they were clearly worried about her. But when she called the young woman to see how she was, she still insisted she was fine, and she sent Liz flowers the next morning at the office, which stunned her. The card read "Don't worry, we're both going to be okay." Liz called Victoria as soon as she got them.

"You must have hit an angel," Victoria said in disbelief. "All of my clients would have sued you for emotional distress, brain damage, spinal injuries, and I'd have collected ten million dollars for them."

"Thank God you retired." Liz laughed for the first time since it had happened. There was nothing to laugh about these days.

"You're damn right. And damn lucky. Now

are you going to stay off the road for a while?"
She was genuinely worried about her.

"I can't. I've got too much to do."

"Well, you'd better be careful. Take this as a
warning."

"I will."

She was exceptionally cautious after that, but
it sobered her a little, and made her realize how
distraught and out of touch she was. And for the
next month, she made a bigger effort to cheer up
for the children. She took them to the movies on
weekends, went bowling with them, encouraged
them to invite their friends for dinner and the
night. And by St. Patrick's Day, another of Jack's
favorite holidays, they weren't in great spirits, but
they were better. It was nearly three months, and
the children at least seemed to be happier, even
Jamie. There was laughter at the dinner table
again, they played their music as loud as they ever
had, and although their faces were still too serious from time to time, she knew that they had
turned the corner. But her nights were still long
and dark and lonely, and her days filled with
stress at the office.

But on Easter weekend, she surprised them.
She couldn't stand the thought of another dismal
holiday, filled with memories of Jack, wandering
the house in agony and trying to overcome it. She

took them all skiing at Lake Tahoe, and the kids really loved it. They looked relieved to see her back out in the world with them, skiing with them, and laughing as she raced Megan down the bunny slope, or collided with Jamie. They all loved it. It had been just what they needed.

And on the drive home, they talked about the summer.

"That's months away, Mom," Annie complained. She had a crush on a boy close to home, and didn't even want to think about going away that summer. Peter already had a summer job lined up, at a nearby veterinary hospital, which wasn't a career path for him, but at least it would keep him busy. And all she had to do was organize the three girls and Jamie.

"I can only get away for a week this year, I've got too much to do now that I'm working alone. How about camp for a month for the three of you? Jamie can stay home with me and do day camp."

"Can I bring my own lunch?" Jamie asked, looking concerned, and Liz smiled at him. He had hated the lunches at the last day camp he went to, but he loved the kids and the activities and she thought it would do him good. He couldn't go away to sleepover camp like his sisters.

"You can bring your own lunch," Liz promised, and he beamed.

"Then I want to go."

Two down. Three to deal with, Liz thought to herself as they drove home from Tahoe. The other three discussed it all the way to Sacramento and decided that camp sounded like a good idea after all. In July. And Liz said she'd take them all to Tahoe for a week in August, and then they could hang around at home, and use the pool with their friends.

"Are we going to give our Fourth of July picnic this year?" It was an annual tradition that Jack organized every year. He did the barbecue, ran the bar, and was a one-man band. Just thinking about it depressed her. There was a long silence and Liz shook her head. No one argued with her, and then as she glanced over at him, she saw that there were two tears sneaking down Jamie's cheeks as she watched him.

"Are you sad about the picnic?" she asked softly, but he shook his head. It was something else. Something much more important.

"I just remembered. Now I can't do Special Olympics." It was an event he loved, that Jack had done with him. They had "trained" for months, and Jamie usually came in last, or close to it, in whatever events he entered, but he always won a ribbon of some kind, and the whole family went to watch him.

"Why can't you?" Liz refused to be daunted. She knew how much Jack had put into it, and how much it meant to Jamie. "Maybe Peter can train with you."

"I can't, Mom," Peter said regretfully. "I'm going to be working from 8 a.m. to 8 p.m. at the pet hospital, and I'll even have to work some weekends." But it was great money, which was why he had agreed to do it. "I won't have time." There was a long, long pause, as the tears continued to roll silently down Jamie's cheeks, and Liz felt as though her heart had been ripped out of her chest as she watched him.

"Okay, Jamie," she said quietly, "that leaves you and me. We'll have to work on this together. We'll figure out what events you want to be in and qualify for, and we'll work our asses off, and this year," she said, fighting back her own tears, "I think we ought to go for a gold medal." Jamie's eyes grew wide at the words.

"Without Daddy?" Jamie looked startled as he turned to see if she meant it or was just teasing. But she wouldn't have done that to him.

"With me. How about it? Let's shoot for the stars."

"You can't, Mom. You don't know how to do it."

"We'll learn together. You can show me what Daddy used to do. And we'll win something, I promise." A slow smile dawned on Jamie's face, and he reached out a hand and touched hers, without saying another word. They had solved the problem. And the summer was organized. All she had to do now was enroll the girls at camp, sign Jamie up for day camp and Special Olympics, and reserve rooms or a house for them in Tahoe for a week in August. It wasn't easy, any of it, figuring it out, meeting their needs single-handedly, living up to their expectations, trying to make up to them for what they had lost, but she was doing her best, and for the moment they were surviving.

They were all doing decent work in school, they smiled a good part of the time now, they'd had a great time skiing with her, and all she had to do now was keep them on track till they grew up, carry a double load in their law practice, and learn how to get Jamie through Special Olympics, and with luck, even win a ribbon. She felt like a juggler in a circus act, as they drove home toward San Francisco, and Megan turned the radio on full blast. But it was familiar at least. Jack would have had a fit over it, and made her turn it off. But Liz didn't. She knew it was a good sign, and they needed all the good signs they could grab now. There had been damn few of them in the past three and a half months, but things were slowly beginning to look up. Liz glanced at Megan with a small smile, and as their eyes met, Liz turned the radio up even slightly louder. And as Megan watched her do it, she started to laugh, and so did her mother.

"Yeah, Mom . . . go for it!!!" They all laughed and shouted and started to sing with the music. It was deafening. But it was just what they needed, and Liz spoke as loud as she could in the din.

"I love you guys!" They managed to hear her despite the noise, and in unison they shouted back to the woman who had guided them over the reefs and back into safe waters, and they knew it, just as she did.

"We love you too, Mom!!!" Their ears were still ringing from the music when they got home, but they were all smiling, as they picked up their bags and walked into the house, and Liz was walking right behind them, smiling.

Carole was waiting for them at the door. "How was it?" she asked, referring to the ski trip as much as the long drive home, and Liz smiled at her with a look of peace Carole hadn't seen on her face in months.

"Terrific," Liz said quietly, and walked up the stairs to her bedroom.

Chapter 5

The kids got out of school on the second week of June, and two weeks later, Liz and Carole were packing their bags for camp. The girls were genuinely excited and several of their friends were going too. It was nice to see them all looking so happy. The camp they were going to was near Monterey, Liz drove them down herself, and took Jamie with her for the trip.

There was a real holiday atmosphere in the car, on the way. They played a variety of CD's, all of them loud, wild, and their kind of music, rather than their mother's. But Liz didn't mind. In the last month or two, she had really enjoyed being with her children. And she had promised Jamie she'd start training with him as soon as the girls left for camp. They had another five weeks before the Special Olympics, and his sisters would be back by then. The whole family always went to the Special Olympics to cheer for Jamie. It was a tradition Jack had started three years before, and one that was important to them. But Jamie was still worried that his mother wouldn't know how to do it with him.

They dropped the girls off at camp between Monterey and Carmel, and Liz helped carry their sleeping bags, tennis rackets, one guitar, two trunks, and a mountain of duffel bags and tote bags to their cabins. It looked like enough gear for an invading army. And they scarcely remembered to kiss her and Jamie good-bye before they ran off to meet their counselors, and find their friends.

"Maybe you'll go to camp one day," Liz said to Jamie as they drove away.

"I don't want to," he said matter-of-factly. "I like being home with you." He looked up at her as he said it, and she smiled at him as they got back on the freeway. It took them three hours to get back to Tiburon, and when they arrived, Peter had just come home from work. He had started the week before, and was loving it, despite the long hours. It was exactly what he wanted. And there were two other high school kids working there that summer too, one of them a very pretty girl from Mill Valley, and a young college intern, from the veterinary college at Davis.

"How was work today?" she asked her oldest son, as she and Jamie walked into the kitchen.

"Busy." He smiled at his mother.

"How about some dinner?"

She was cooking for them again, as she had been for months. Carole had covered for her before that. But ever since Easter, she felt as though she had reconnected with her children. Her mother was still calling regularly to check on her, but even her predictions of doom didn't seem quite as ominous. It was beginning to seem as though they were going to make it after all. She was managing at work, despite an enormous workload. She had finished all of Jack's cases, and started some new ones on her own. The kids were in good shape. The summer was off to a reasonable start. And she still missed Jack, but she could get through the days, and even the nights now. She didn't sleep as well as she once had, but she was asleep by two now instead of five, and most of the time, she was in fairly decent spirits. Though occasionally, she still had some real sinkers, and some intensely down days. But now at last there were plenty of good ones too, more than bad.

She made pasta and salad that night for the three of them, and ice cream sundaes, and Jamie helped her make them. He put the whipped cream on, and the nuts, and the maraschino cherries.

"Just like in a restaurant," Jamie announced, proud of himself, as he served them.

"Have you and Mom started training for the Olympics yet?" Peter asked with interest as he demolished the sundae.

"We start tomorrow," their mother answered.

"What events are you entering this year?" Peter talked to him now like a father, more than just an older brother. He had picked up the slack wherever possible, and had even finished the year with fairly respectable grades, in spite of everything that had happened. And in the fall, he'd be a senior. Liz was planning to visit colleges with him in September. Mostly up and down the West Coast. He didn't want to go far from home now, although before his father had died he'd been talking about Princeton and Yale and Harvard. But now he was looking toward UCLA, and Berkeley, and Stanford.

"I'm going to do the running long jump, and the hundred yard dash . . . and the sack race," Jamie said proudly. "I was going to do the egg toss again, but Mom says I'm too old now."

"Sounds good to me. I'll bet you win another ribbon," Peter said with a warm smile, as Liz watched them both with a look of pleasure. They were both good boys, and she was glad they were at home with her. She enjoyed their company, and she could concentrate on them with the girls gone.

"Mom thinks I'll win first prize this time," Jamie said, but he didn't look convinced. He still wasn't sure how adept his mother would be as a trainer. He was used to practicing with his father.

"I'll bet you do too," Peter said, helping himself to more ice cream, and giving some to his little brother.

"I don't mind winning last place," Jamie said matter-of-factly, "just so I get a ribbon."

"Thanks for your faith in me as a trainer." Liz smiled at her youngest son, and started clearing the dishes, and then she told him to get ready for bed. Jamie was starting day camp in the morning.

And the next day when she drove him there on the way to work, she looked at Jamie proudly and leaned over to give him a kiss. "I love you, kiddo. Have fun. I'll be home at six, and we'll start practicing for the Olympics."

He nodded and blew her a kiss as he got out of the car, and she headed for the office. It was a warm, sunny day in Marin, though she could see fog stretched across the bridge, and she knew it was probably cool in San Francisco. It was a pretty summer day, and she thought of Jack suddenly, with a quick knife stab in the heart. She still had them sometimes, when she thought of him, or saw something they had both loved or done together. But she felt better again by the time she got to the office. But no matter what she did, or how busy she was, she still missed him.

"Any messages?" she asked Jean as she walked in, and Jean handed her seven little slips of paper. Two were from new clients she had just met the week before, two were from attorneys she had referred cases to, two were from people she didn't know, and one was from her mother.

She returned all her business calls, and then called her mother.

"Did the girls get off to camp all right?"

"Perfectly. I took them down yesterday, Jamie started day camp this morning, and Peter is working."

"What about you, Liz? What are you doing about getting on with your life?"

"This is my life, Mom. I'm taking care of my kids, and working." What else did she expect her to do now?

"That's not enough for a woman your age. You're forty-one years old, you're still young, but not young enough to be wasting time. You should be dating." Oh, for God's sake. It was the last thing on her mind. She was still wearing her wedding band, and similar inquiries by friends had been rebuffed promptly. She had no interest whatsoever in dating. In her heart, she still felt married to Jack, and felt as though she always would be.

"It's only been six months, Mom. Besides, I'm too busy."

"Some people are remarried by then. Six months is a long time."

"So is nineteen years. What's new with you? Are *you* dating?"

"I'm too old for that," her mother snapped at her, although they both knew she wasn't. "You know what I'm saying." Sell the house. Close the office. Find a husband. Her mother had lots of good advice to give her, or so she thought, as did everyone else Liz knew. Everyone had some kind of advice to give her, and she wasn't buying. "When are you going to take a vacation?"

"In August. I'm taking the kids to Tahoe."

"Good. You need it."

"Thank you. I'd better get to work. I've got a lot to do this morning." She wanted to get off the phone before her mother got on her case about something else. There was always something.

"Have you put away Jack's things yet?"

Christ. It was hopeless. "No, I haven't. I don't need the space."

"You need the healing, Liz, and you know it."

"So how come Daddy's coats are still in your downstairs closet?"

"That's different. I have nowhere else to store them." Store them for whom? And for what? They both knew it was no different.

"I'm not ready to put them away, Mom." And maybe I never will be, she acknowledged to herself in silence. She didn't want him out of her life or her head or her heart, or her closets. She wasn't ready to say good-bye yet.

"You're not going to get better till you do that."

"I am better. Much better. I've got to go now."

"You just don't want to hear it, but you know I'm right." Who says so? Who says I have to put his things away? She felt the familiar knife-stab of pain again that she had already felt once that morning. Her mother was definitely not helping.

"I'll call you this weekend," she promised her mother.

"Don't work too hard, Liz. I still think you should close the office."

"I may have to if you don't let me get to work, Mom."

"All right, all right. I'll talk to you on Sunday."

After she hung up, Liz sat staring out the window, thinking of Jack, and what her mother had said, but it was just too painful to let go and do the things her mother had suggested. It was comforting to still see his clothes hanging in his closet. Sometimes she'd let herself touch a sleeve wistfully, or sniff the cologne that still lingered on his collars. She had finally put his shaving gear away, and thrown away his toothbrush. But she couldn't bring herself to do more than that. The rest of it was all there, and she liked it. And one day, when she didn't like it anymore, she would do something about it. But hopefully, not for a long time. She wasn't ready, and she knew it.

"Are you okay?" Jean had walked into the room and saw her staring out the window with a look of sorrow. But Liz stirred quickly when she heard her, and looked at her with a wistful smile.

"My mother. She always has some piece of advice to give me."

"Mothers are like that. You have court this afternoon, I assume you remember."

"I do. Though I can't say I'm looking forward to it." She had maintained their practice exactly as it had been. She was still taking all the same cases that Jack would have approved of, and wanted to fight. She was still using the same criteria for accepting them, and referring the same ones that Jack wouldn't have wanted. She was doing it for him, and still respecting the guidelines he had set for them, but there were times when she questioned what she was doing. There was so much about family law that she didn't like, so many of the battles that seemed unimportant to her. And dealing with people who hated each other, were so willing to hit below the belt and hurt each other, and constantly cause each other trouble and pain, was beginning to depress her, and Jean knew that. Liz's heart wasn't in it the way it had been when Jack was alive. They had been great as a team, but on her own, she just didn't have the fire she'd once had anymore. She wouldn't have admitted it to anyone, but the constant irritations of dealing with divorce had begun to bore her.

But no one would have guessed that when she walked into court that afternoon. As usual, she was well prepared, totally organized, and fought valiantly for her client, and easily won the motion. It was a trivial point, but she handled it to perfection, and the judge thanked her for her rapid disposal of a relatively small matter that the opposing counsel was frivolously trying to turn into a major issue.

It was nearly five o'clock when she got back to the office, answered a few more calls, and gathered up her things. She wanted to be home by five-thirty for Jamie.

"Are you leaving?" Jean walked in with a stack of papers for her that had just been delivered from another attorney's office. The material was part of the discovery in a new divorce case, and came from a well-known firm in the city.

"I have to get home to train with Jamie. He's going to be in the Special Olympics again this year."

"That's nice, Liz," Jean said smiling. She was carrying on all of Jack's traditions, holding high the standard of his memory, for her clients, herself, and her children. It was obvious she didn't want anything to change, and so far, it hadn't. Every minute piece of her life was still in exactly the same place it had been before she lost her husband. She didn't even sit at his desk now, or use his office, although she had always liked his better. She had simply closed his door, and rarely went into his office anymore, and there was no one else to use it. It was as though she still expected him to come back one day, and sit there. At first, Jean had thought it was eerie, but by now she was used to it. They only went in there from time to time, to get some papers. But most of their active files were now in Liz's office.

"See you tomorrow," Liz said, as she hurried out the door. And when she got home, Jamie was waiting for her. She ran into the house, changed into jeans and a sweatshirt, and running shoes, and five minutes later, she was back outside again, and going over the running long jump with Jamie. The first time he tried it, his performance was pretty unimpressive, and he knew it.

"I can't do it." He looked defeated before he started, and as though he wanted to give up, but she wouldn't let him.

"Yes, you can. Watch me." She showed him, and tried to do it slowly so he could see it. He was more visual than auditory and he did a little better the next time. "Try it again," she encouraged him, and after a while Carole came out to them with a glass of Gatorade and a plate of freshly baked chocolate chip cookies.

"How's it going?" she asked cheerfully, and Jamie shook his head, looking mournful.

"Not good. I'm not going to win a ribbon."

"Yes, you are," Liz said firmly. She wanted him to win, because she knew how much it meant to him, and he had always won one when he trained with his father. After he ate two cookies and drank half the Gatorade, she told him to try it again, and this time he did better. And she reminded him of the Special Olympics oath "Let me win, but if I cannot win, let me be brave in the attempt."

They continued practicing for a while, and then she had him do a dash across the yard and timed him. He was better at the dash than the long jump, he always had been. Running was his strong suit, he was faster than most of the kids he ran against, and better able to focus on what he was doing. Despite his handicaps, he had a surprising amount of concentration, and he had even finally learned to read that winter, and he was very proud of it. He read everything he could get his hands on. Cereal boxes, mustard labels, milk cartons, storybooks, flyers that people stuck under her windshield, even letters that Liz left on the kitchen table. At ten, he loved the fact that he could read now.

At seven o'clock, Liz suggested they call it a day, but he wanted to keep working at it for a while, and she finally talked him into going inside at seven-thirty.

"We still have a month to train, sweetheart. We don't have to do it all in one night."

"Dad always said I had to do it till I couldn't stand up anymore. I can still stand up," he said simply and she smiled at him.

"I think we should quit for the night while you're still standing. We can do it again tomorrow."

"Okay," he finally conceded. He had worked hard and he was exhausted, and when they walked back into the kitchen, Carole had dinner ready for them. It was roast chicken and mashed potatoes, with glazed carrots, one of Jamie's favorite dinners. And a hot apple pie fresh out of the oven.

"Yum!" he said with a look of delight, and he gobbled up everything on his plate while he chatted about the Olympics with his mother. He was genuinely excited about it.

He took a bath and went to bed right after dinner. He had to get up early for day camp, and she had some work to do. She took her briefcase upstairs and kissed him good night, and then set her briefcase down in her bedroom, and walked into her closet. They had a big walk-in closet that Jack had built for them. She used one side, and Jack's clothes hung on the other. And remembering what her mother had said on the phone that morning, she found herself looking at his things again, with more longing than she had in a while. It felt like everyone was trying to take them from her, and she wasn't ready to give them up, or forget him.

She found herself running a hand over his jackets again, and she held one of them to her face and smelled it. It still smelled of him. She wondered if his clothes always would, or if eventually the scent of him would fade away. She couldn't bear the thought of it, and she felt her eyes fill with tears as she buried her face in one of his jackets. She didn't hear Peter come in, and she jumped when she suddenly felt a hand on her shoulder, turned and saw him.

"You shouldn't do that, Mom," he said softly, watching her, with tears in his own eyes.

"Why not?" She was crying then, and he reached out and held her in his arms. He was not only her son, but her friend now. At seventeen, he had grown into manhood instantly when he lost his father. "I still miss him so much," she confessed to him, and he nodded.

"I know. But doing this doesn't change anything. It doesn't help. It just makes it worse. I used to come in here too, and do the same thing, but it made me so sad I stopped. Maybe you should pack up his stuff. If you want, I'll help you," Peter offered.

"Grandma said I should too. . . . I just don't want to," Liz said sadly.

"Then don't. Do it when you're ready."

"What if I never am?"

"You will be. You'll know when." He held her for a long moment, and then she slowly pulled away and smiled up at him. The moment of sheer agony had passed, and she felt better as she looked at her son. He was a good boy, and she loved him more than she could tell him, just as she loved all her kids.

"I love you, Mom."

"I love you too, sweetheart. Thanks for being there for me, and for all the others." He nodded, and they walked back into her room again, as she glanced at her briefcase. For once, she just didn't feel like working. Doing what she had just done, trying to hold on to Jack, by clinging to his clothes, and smelling his cologne on them, always made her feel worse after the initial indulgence. The positive aspects only lasted for a few seconds. But she only missed him more afterwards. It was what Peter had discovered, and why he had stopped doing the same thing, just as he had told her.

"Why don't you give yourself a breather tonight, just take a hot bath, or go to a movie or something," he said wisely.

"I've got work to do."

"You always have work to do. It'll wait. If Dad were here, he'd take you out. Even he didn't work every night the way you do now."

"No, but he worked at home a lot. More than I did then."

"You can't be you and him, Mom. All you can be is you. It's too much to do both parts."

"When did you get so wise?" She smiled at him as he stood in the doorway, but they both knew the answer to that. Peter had grown up about six months before, on Christmas morning. He had had to do it very quickly, to help her and his siblings. There was no choice now. Even the girls had grown up a lot in the last six months, and despite her awkward age, Megan was always offering to help her. Liz knew she was going to miss her while she was at camp, but they deserved to get away and have a good time. They all did.

Peter went to his own room then, and in her room, Liz sat down on her bed and spread out her papers. She was still working long after Peter had gone to bed. She always worked late now. She hated to go to bed, or to try and sleep. It was always a battle to fight the memories out of her head. The nights were a lot harder than the days, and had been from the beginning.

But by two she was finally asleep, and by seven, she was up and running. She dropped Jamie off at camp again, went to work, sifted through her caseload, dictated letters to Jean, made a dozen phone calls, and at five-thirty she was back in the backyard, timing Jamie's dashes. In its own way, it was a pleasant treadmill. Kids, work, kids, work, sleep, and then the same routine all over again. For the moment, it was all she had, and all she wanted.

By the time camp was over for the girls, Jamie had picked up a lot of speed on his dashes, and improved his distance on the running long jump. They had even practiced the sack race, with a burlap bag she had gotten at the feed store. He was gaining in confidence as well as speed. And he made up in effort and goodwill what he lacked in coordination.

But Jamie was even more excited about seeing his sisters when they came home than he was about the Special Olympics. And they were thrilled to see him. Jamie was special to all of them. And the day before camp ended for the girls, Liz took Jamie and a friend to Marine World. He loved getting splashed by the dolphins and the whales. He was absolutely soaked by the time they left and got in the car to drive home. Liz had to wrap him in towels so he didn't catch cold, and he was ecstatic about the day.

The Special Olympics were scheduled for the following weekend. Liz trained every night with him, and all morning the day before the event. And when his sisters watched him, they applauded and cheered. He was better than he had ever been, and the night before he could hardly sleep he was so excited. He slept in Liz's bed that night, as he still did fairly often. She never complained about it, or discouraged him, because selfishly she loved it too, and it gave them both comfort.

The morning of the Olympics was sunny and warm, and she and Jamie left before the others. Peter was going to drive over an hour later with Carole and the girls. Liz was carrying Jack's videocamera, and wearing her Nikon. They checked in at the gate of the fairgrounds, and Jamie was given a number. There were children like him everywhere, and many far more challenged than he, many of them seemed severely afflicted, and there were endless numbers of kids in wheel-chairs. It was a familiar sight to Liz, and it touched her to see how happy they all were, and how excited. Jamie could hardly wait for his first event, and as they lined up for the hundred yard dash, he suddenly turned to his mother with a look of panic.

"I can't," he said in a choked voice. "I can't, Mom."

"Yes, you can," she said quietly, holding his hand. "You know you can, Jamie. It doesn't mat-ter if you win, it's just for fun, sweetheart. All you have to do is have a good time. That's all, just try to relax and enjoy it."

"I can't do it without Daddy." She hadn't been prepared for that, and her eyes filled with tears as he said it.

"Daddy would want you to have a good time. This means a lot to you, and it did for him. It'll make you feel good if you win a ribbon." She spoke in a quavering voice, fighting back tears, but for once, Jamie didn't see them.

"I don't want to without him," he said, burst-ing into tears of his own, and burying his head in his mother's chest, and for a minute she wondered if she should let him drop out, or encourage him to do it. But it was like everything else they had to face now, unbearably hard the first time, but once they got through the pain, there was a sense of victory to have survived it.

"Why don't you try one event," Liz reasoned with him, as she kept her arms around him and stroked his hair, "and if you hate it, we'll just watch from the stands, or go home if you want. Just do this one." He hesitated for a long time, and said nothing, as they called the participants in the dash to the starting line, and then he looked up at her and nodded. She walked to the starting line with him, and he turned and looked at her for a long time, and then he lined up with the others. She blew him a kiss before he turned around, something Jack would never have done. Jack always treated him like a man, and he always said she treated Jamie like a baby. But he was her baby, and no matter how grown up he eventually got, or how capable, he always would be.

She stood watching him with tears in her eyes as he ran, and shouting encouragement with the other parents. But she wanted him to win this time, for himself, for Jack, and to prove that things were still all right, that he could live on without his father. Jamie needed this even more than the others, and maybe in some small way, she did also. She watched, holding her breath as he approached the finish line. He looked as though he might come in third or fourth, and then with a sudden burst, he pulled ahead of the others. He didn't look to either side, or glance around, as some of the others did, he just pushed himself as hard as he could and kept going, and then with a look of astonishment, as tears streamed down her face, she realized that he had come in first. The ribbon had snapped across his chest, and he was panting at the other end, and looking around wildly for her as the official "hugger" gave Jamie a big hug and congratulated him. There were scores of volunteers who did just that. Liz ran to him as fast as she could, and he threw his arms around her when he saw her.

"I won! I won! I came in first! . . . I won, Mom! I never did that with Daddy!" But Jack would have been so pleased for him, and so proud of him, and Liz could just imagine him smiling at them. She was holding Jamie close to her, and thanking God and Jack for making it happen for him, she kissed the top of Jamie's head and told him how proud of him she was, and he looked surprised when he glanced up and saw that she was crying. "Aren't you happy, Mom?" He looked confused and she laughed.

"You bet I am!! You were fantastic!!" They both waved to Peter and the girls in the stands, and made a victory sign, and Peter and the girls stood up and cheered when they announced the winner of the hundred yard dash on the P.A. system as Jamie was getting his gold medal off to the side. No matter what else happened that day, Jamie had won.

He came in second in the running long jump after that, and won a silver medal, and tied for first in the sack race. By the end of the day, he'd won two gold medals and a silver, and he'd never been as happy in his life, when they finally drove home late that afternoon as he sat in the car with all three medals around his neck. It had been a wonderful day, full of excitement and victories and tender moments. And Liz took them all out to dinner at the Buckeye in Sausalito to celebrate. It was a day they would long remember and all be proud of.

"I never did that with Dad," Jamie said again over dinner. "You're a really good trainer, Mom. I didn't think you could do it."

"Neither did I," Megan said proudly, looking at her mother. And Rachel and Annie teased him about what a hot athlete he was, while Liz said she was going to frame the medals for him.

"You did a great job, Mom," Annie complimented her.

"Jamie did the hard part. All I did was time him in the backyard. That was pretty easy." But they had done it every day for five weeks running, and it had paid off. Jamie had never been as happy in his life, or as proud. He showed everyone near them in the restaurant his ribbons and medals. And when Liz tucked him into bed that night, he thanked her again, and put his arms around her neck, and pulled her closer.

"I love you, Mommy. I miss Daddy, but I love you a lot."

"You're a great boy, and I love you, Jamie. I miss Daddy too, but I think he was watching you today and he was really proud of you."

"I think so too," Jamie said with a yawn, and she scratched his back for a minute when he turned on his side. He was asleep before she ever left his bedroom. And she was still smiling to herself as she walked back to her own room. Peter had gone out by then, and he had taken Megan with him to a movie. Rachel and Annie were watching a video, and Liz walked quietly into her room, thinking about her husband.

"We did it," she whispered in the dark. And as she looked around the empty room, she could almost feel him. It was a presence, and a force, and a love that was not easily forgotten. "Thank you," she said softly as she turned on the light, but she no longer expected to see him, or him to come back. But what he had left her with was infinitely precious.

Chapter 6

They left for Tahoe three days after the Special Olympics. And Jamie was still in high spirits. They all were. An old friend of Jack's had lent her his house in Homewood. It was a rambling old house they'd borrowed from him before. His wife didn't like Tahoe, his kids were grown, and they seldom used it. And it was perfect for Liz and the children. It had a wide, sheltered porch, and you could see the lake from most of the bedrooms. It was surrounded by five acres of land. There were big, beautiful trees, and everyone was in a great mood when they got there.

Peter and the girls helped Liz get everything out of the car, and Jamie took the groceries into the house and helped her unpack them. Carole had gone to Santa Barbara for a week to stay with her sister.

"What about a swim?" Peter suggested almost as soon as they arrived. And half an hour later, they were all jumping off the nearby dock, shivering in the cold water. But that was part of the fun of it, and Liz had arranged for them to go waterskiing the next morning.

She cooked dinner for them that night, and Peter helped with the barbecue. His father had taught him how to do it. And they sat in front of the fireplace afterwards, telling stories and roasting marshmallows. And after a while, Annie told a funny story about their father. Liz smiled as she listened, and it reminded her of another time, and another story. She told it, and they all laughed, and then Rachel reminded them of when Dad had accidentally locked himself into a cabin they'd rented and had to climb out the window. And after a while it was a contest of who could remember the silliest stories. It was a way of bringing him back to them, in a way they could all tolerate now. The months that had passed had taken the edge off the pain for them, and left them with not just the tears, but the laughter.

And when they all finally went upstairs to go to bed, Liz felt better than she had in months. She still missed him, but she wasn't quite as sad, and they were all happy to be there. It was a vacation they all needed, and she was glad that Peter had managed to get the time off to come with them. He was doing such a good job at the pet hospital that they had given him the week off and told him to enjoy it.

They all went waterskiing the next day, and Peter took Rachel and Jamie fishing in the stream behind the house, and they caught a fish. And the next day they took out the small boat that was tied to the dock, and both boys caught fish, and then Megan landed a big one. They caught crawdads near the dock, and Liz cooked them that night for dinner. It was an easy, happy time for all of them, and they slept on the porch one night in sleeping bags, and looked up at the stars. It was a perfect vacation.

And when they packed their things at the end of the week, they were all genuinely sorry to leave, and made Liz promise to do it again that summer. She thought they might borrow the house again on Labor Day. It was a way of avoiding the party they always gave then. Like the Fourth of July picnic they had decided not to give this year, their end of summer party on Labor Day was a family tradition. But going to Lake Tahoe instead was an ideal substitute for it.

They were all relaxed and happy when they drove home the next day, and stopped at Ikeda's in Auburn for hamburgers and milk shakes.

"I hate to go back to work," Liz confessed to her oldest son as they both finished their milk shakes. "This was so much fun, I wish I could be lazy for the rest of the summer."

"Why don't you take some more time off, Mom?" he suggested, and she shook her head. She could just imagine what was waiting for her now at the office, she had court appearances scheduled all through the month, and a trial in early September she had to prepare for.

"I'm swamped."

"You work too hard, Mom." But they both knew she was still trying to carry her own load and his father's. "Why don't you hire another lawyer to help you?"

"I've thought about it. But somehow I think your father wouldn't have liked that."

"He wouldn't have wanted you to kill yourself working this hard either." Jack had always known how to have a good time, and as compulsive as he was about their work, no one liked a vacation better than he did. He would have loved the week they had just spent at Lake Tahoe.

"I'll see. Maybe in a few months I'll bring another lawyer into the practice. But so far, I'm doing okay by myself." As long as she never stopped to read a book or a magazine, or have lunch with a friend or get her hair done. As long as she kept her nose to the grindstone every minute she wasn't with the kids, it worked fine, but it wasn't much of a life for her, and she knew it. And apparently, so did her children.

"Don't wait forever, Mom," Peter admonished her, and rounded the others up. They were buying candy, and carried bags of it back to the car to take home with them. It was part of the charm of Ikeda's. It was one of their favorite stops. They usually stopped there too on their way to ski at Tahoe in the winter.

Carole was waiting for them when they got home, and Liz knew that the next few weeks would be busy for her, before the kids went back to school. Peter would still be working at the pet hospital for another week or two, but the others would be spending all their time around the pool, and inviting friends over to hang out with them. Carole would fix lunch for half a dozen kids or more every day, and sometimes twice that many at dinner. But Liz liked knowing where they were, and that their friends were welcome to visit.

Carole had cooked a delicious dinner for them, and when they went to bed that night, they were happy to be home, and full of stories of the lake to tell her. And Liz still looked relaxed when she left for work the next morning. It lasted for all of about ten minutes. The stacks of work and files on her desk had multiplied dramatically while she was gone, and there were more phone messages than she had ever seen waiting for her. She was handling her cases too well. Both clients and other attorneys were constantly referring new cases to her. And she couldn't help but remember what Peter had said about taking another lawyer into the practice to help her.

She mentioned it to Jean that afternoon as they attacked her desk systematically, and Liz did some dictation.

"Do you have anyone in mind?" Jean asked with interest. She'd been thinking the same thing herself for quite a while, and applauded Peter for the astute suggestion.

"Not yet," Liz admitted to her. "I don't even know if I want to do it."

"You should give it some thought. He's right. You can't do it all yourself. It's too much for one person. It was almost too much for two before Jack died, and the practice has grown in the last six months. I don't know if you've noticed it, but I have. You're handling twice as many cases than you were when there were two of you to do them."

"How did that happen?" Liz looked surprised as she acknowledged what Jean was saying.

"You're good at what you do, that's how," Jean said with a smile.

"So was Jack." Liz was quick to defend him. "I always thought he was a better lawyer than I was."

"I wouldn't say that," Jean said honestly, "but he turned away more cases than you do. You never have the heart to say no to anyone. If he didn't like a case, he booted it right out the door into the hands of some other lawyer."

"Maybe I should do more of that," she said thoughtfully.

"I'm not sure you could bring yourself to do it." Jean knew her well. Liz was incredibly conscientious.

"Neither am I," Liz said as she laughed, and they went back to work on the dictation. She had a number of things to send to various judges, and other attorneys, on the cases she was currently working on.

It was late when she got home that night, nearly eight o'clock, but she was paying her dues for her vacation. The kids were still sitting around the pool when she got home, and Carole was dishing out pizza.

"Hi, guys," Liz said with a smile, and she was pleased to see Peter there, but less so when she saw two of his friends dive into the pool and play a little too roughly with the younger children when they all got into a game of Marco Polo. She told them to tone it down a little bit, and asked

Peter to tell his friends not to play quite so roughly. "Someone's going to get hurt," she said quietly to Carole, who agreed with her and said she had spent the whole afternoon telling Megan's friends the same thing. Liz was particularly worried about Jamie, who was only a fair swimmer.

And she warned them about it again that night after their friends left. "I don't want any accidents here . . . or any lawsuits!"

"You worry too much, Mom." Annie dismissed her, and Liz told her that she meant it.

She reminded them of it again the next day when she left for work, and when she came home that night, things seemed a little calmer. But on Thursday, when she came home late again, and found half a dozen of Peter's friends in the pool with him, she watched them diving too fast, too soon, and not waiting until the other children had cleared the area, and she told him in no uncertain terms that his friends would be banned from the pool if they didn't observe basic safety rules, and respect the younger children.

"I don't want to have to remind you again," she said sternly.

"You look tired, Mom," he said gently.

"I am tired, but that's beside the point. I don't want an accident here. You can't roughhouse in the pool, Peter, and I mean it."

"Okay, Mom, I heard you." He had grown up a lot in the past year, but not completely. He was still young, and some of his friends were daredevils and foolish, and she had always worried about it. Having someone get hurt was a headache she didn't need. They'd been through enough trauma for one year, and she wasn't afraid to say so to him, or his friends.

She went up to her room to work again that night, and she had an early appearance in court the next morning. She was tired and edgy, and she wanted to get a good night's sleep.

She was just leaving the courtroom in fact, at noon the next day, when her cellular rang. It was Carole, and she sounded precise and calm, as Liz stopped to talk to her on the steps of the courthouse.

"You need to come home right away," she said clearly, and Liz felt her spine tense. Carole only sounded like that when one of the kids got hurt, or there was a serious problem.

"What happened? Is someone hurt?" She knew before Carole told her.

"It's Peter. He had a day off from work, and some of his friends were here." Liz interrupted her instantly in a shrill tone that was unfamiliar to her own ears, but her nerves were no longer what they once had been.

"What happened?"

"We don't know yet. He was diving and he hit his head, I think. The ambulance is here."

"Is he bleeding?" All she could think of was Jack as he lay on their office floor with blood everywhere. If there was blood, to her now it meant disaster.

"No," Carole said with a calm she didn't feel. She had hated to be the one to tell her, but she knew she had to. "He's unconscious." She didn't have the heart to tell her he might have broken his neck. They weren't sure yet. "They're taking him to Marin General. You can meet him there. Liz, I'm sorry."

"Is everyone else okay?" She was running to the car as she asked her.

"No one else was hurt. Just Peter."

"Is he going to be okay?"

No one really knew. There were paramedics everywhere, and Liz could hear the sirens start to wail as they took off with him as she asked the question.

"I think so. I don't know much, Liz. I was watching them . . . I told them. . . ." Carole started to cry as she said it, and Liz started her car, and ended the conversation as she pulled away from the curb, praying that he'd be all right. He had to be. They couldn't live through another disaster, or God forbid, losing him. She just couldn't. She drove to the hospital as fast as she could without running lights or hitting pedestrians, and she pulled into the parking lot shortly after they rushed Peter into the emergency room. They had taken him straight to the trauma unit, and they directed Liz to it as soon as she got there.

She was running down the halls, looking for him, and as soon as she walked into the trauma unit, she saw him. He was gray and wet and they were giving him oxygen, and working on him frantically. They were too busy to talk to her, a nurse explained to her rapidly what was happening. He had a severe head injury, and a possible fracture of several vertebrae. They were going to X-ray Peter as soon as possible, and they were running IV lines into him, and putting monitors on him as Liz watched them.

"Is he going to be all right?" Liz asked without taking her eyes off her son, overwhelmed by a wave of panic. He looked like he was dying, and she wasn't sure that he wasn't.

"We don't know yet," the nurse told her honestly. "The doctor will speak to you as soon as they assess him."

Liz wanted to touch him, and talk to him, but she couldn't even get near him. And all she could do was stand there, and wrestle with her own panic. They were bringing an X-ray machine in, they had cut his bathing suit off, and he was lying naked on the gurney.

They X-rayed his head and his neck, and they seemed to be examining every part of him, as his mother watched them. She was crying as she looked at him, and it seemed an eternity before a doctor in green scrubs walked toward her. He had a stethoscope around his neck, and he looked stern as he explained the situation to her. He was tall, and his dark eyes looked grim, but the gray at his temples made her want to believe that he knew what he was doing.

"How is he?" she asked, sounding desperate.

"Not great at the moment. We're not sure yet how bad the head injury is, or what the implications are. There's a broad range of possibilities here. There's a fair amount of internal swelling. We're going to do an EEG, and a CT scan in a few minutes. And a lot is going to depend on how fast he comes out of it. I think he may have gotten lucky with his neck. I thought it was broken when he came in, but I don't think it is. We'll have the X rays back in a minute." He saw a lot of quadriplegics come in from pool accidents, mostly boys this age, in their late teens, who played too rough, or dove without caution. But this kid seemed to have gotten lucky. There was no paralysis of his limbs, and he had good mobility from what they could tell. If anything, he had a hairline fracture, which, five minutes later, is what the X rays told them. He had a hairline fracture of the fourth cervical vertebra, but he hadn't damaged his spinal cord. Now they had to concentrate on his head injuries.

And for just an instant, before they took him away, she was able to reach out and touch him. All she could think of to say to him was "I love you," but Peter was still unconscious and couldn't hear her.

It was nearly an hour later before he came back, and he still looked gray, and the doctor who came to talk to her again didn't look happy. She had learned that he was the head of the trauma unit by then, and his name was Bill Webster.

"Your son has quite a concussion, Mrs. Sutherland. And a hell of a lot of swelling. All we can do is wait now, and if the swelling gets worse, we're going to have to go in and relieve it."

"You mean brain surgery?" She looked horrified, as he nodded. "Will he be . . . is he . . ." She couldn't even formulate the words beyond her panic.

"We don't know yet. There are a lot of variables here. We're going to keep him quiet for a little while and see what happens."

"Can I sit with him?"

"As long as you stay out of our way, and don't

move him. We need him quiet.'' He spoke to her as though she were the enemy, and she felt as though he was. There was a toughness to the man, and a lack of sensitivity, which she hated instantly. But all he was interested in was saving Peter, which slightly redeemed him.

''I won't get in your way,'' she said quietly.

He told her where she could sit, and she pulled up a stool next to where Peter lay, and quietly held his hand. There was an oxygen monitor on one finger, and there were monitors everywhere, to keep track of his heart and his brain waves. For the moment at least, he was stable.

''Where were you when this happened?'' he asked accusingly, and she wanted to slap him.

''In court. I'm a lawyer. My housekeeper was at the pool with them, but I guess things got out of hand.''

''So I gather,'' he said curtly, and went to talk to a resident and another doctor. He came back again a few minutes later. ''We're going to give it another hour or two, and then take him upstairs to surgery,'' he said bluntly, and she nodded. She was sitting on the stool, holding Peter's hand as best she could.

''Can he hear me if I talk to him?''

''It's unlikely,'' he said, looking at her with a frown. She was as pale as her son, but she was also a redhead and very fair. ''Are you all right?'' he asked, and she nodded. "We don't have time to deal with you here if you faint. If this is too much for you, you can sit in the waiting room and we'll call you if anything happens."

"I'm not going anywhere," she said firmly. She had lived through what had happened to Jack eight months before, and she hadn't fainted then. She hated the way this man was speaking to her, but one of the nurses had told her he was the best there was, and she was willing to believe it. But his bedside manner was appalling. He was used to life-and-death situations, and saving lives, his whole focus was on that, and not their relatives. The last thing he wanted was to have to worry about someone other than his patient. He hurried away again, to call a neurosurgeon he wanted available if needed, and a nurse came to ask her if she wanted coffee.

"No, thanks, I'm fine," she said softly, but it was obvious that she wasn't. She looked as desperate as she felt, as worried about her son as she had once been about her husband. And all she knew was that she couldn't lose this time. It was more than she could bear just thinking of it, and every time she did, she leaned over and spoke softly to Peter.

"Come on, Peter . . . wake up . . . talk to me . . . it's Mom . . . open your eyes . . . talk to me . . . it's Mommy, sweetheart . . . I love you . . . Wake up. . . ." It was a mantra she said over and over and over again, praying that wherever he was, in the distant recesses of unconsciousness, he could hear her.

It was two-thirty in the afternoon by then, and at four, nothing had changed, and the doctor came back and talked to her again. They were going to give Peter another hour to regain consciousness on his own, and reassess the situation then. She nodded as she listened. He hadn't stirred since he came in, but she and the doctor both agreed that his color was a little better. The doctor noticed at the same time however that hers wasn't, but he didn't say anything about it. She looked awful. And he mellowed a little bit this time as he spoke to her, but not much. He only asked if she had called the boy's father, and she shook her head, and didn't offer to explain it to him.

"You probably should," he said cautiously, there was something in her eyes that made him hesitate, maybe a bad divorce, or some awkward situation. "He's not out of the woods yet."

"His father died eight months ago," she said finally. "There's no one else to call." She had already called home and told everyone he was still alive but she wouldn't call again until she had more news about his condition. She sounded calmer than she felt. All she could do was pray now that Peter would not join his father. She was praying that the doctor could prevent that.

"I'm sorry," he said, and disappeared again, as she looked intently at her son, and although she would have died before she told anyone, she was beginning to feel the room spin slowly around her. It was all too much for her, too terrible, too terrifying. She couldn't lose him. Couldn't. She wouldn't let him leave them. She put her head down as far as she could, and felt better, and then went back to talking quietly to Peter. And as though he had heard her prayers, he moved ever so slowly, and tried to turn his head, but they had put a neck brace on him and he couldn't. His eyes still didn't open. She started talking to him in a stronger voice then, urging him to open his eyes and talk to her, or blink if he could hear her, squeeze her hand, move his toe, anything. But there was no sign from Peter, until at last he let out a soft moan, but it was impossible to tell if it was a sound he had made unconsciously, or in response to what she was saying to him. And a nurse came running as soon as she heard him. She checked his vital signs again, looked at the monitors, and ran to get the doctor. Liz couldn't tell if it was a good sign or not, but she kept talking to him, and begging him to hear her. And just as the doctor came back again,

Peter moaned again, and this time his eyes fluttered open as she stood next to him, looking down at him with hope and terror.

"Mmmmmmmmmooooommmmmmm . . ." he said in a long agonized sound, but she knew what he had said, and so did Bill Webster. He had said "Mom," though with excruciating effort. And tears were pouring down her cheeks as she leaned closer to him and told him how much she loved him. And when she glanced back at the doctor, much to her amazement, he was smiling.

"We're getting there. Keep talking to him. I want to run some more tests on him." Peter's eyes had closed again, but he opened them as she continued to talk to him, and he let out a horrible moan this time and squeezed her hand almost imperceptibly. But he was coming around, and moving ahead, by millimeters, if nothing more.

"Owwwwwwww," he said, looking at her with a frown. "Owwww . . ." he said again, and she moved toward the doctor.

"He's in pain," she said softly, and Bill Webster nodded.

"I'll bet he is. He's got one hell of a headache." He was putting something in Peter's IV as he spoke to her, and a technician took more blood. And a few minutes later, the neurosurgeon came to see him. "We're getting there," Bill

Webster told him, and looked encouraged. Dr. Webster shared the latest data with him, and they told Liz that they weren't going to do surgery yet. And with luck, and some more progress, maybe they wouldn't have to. It was six o'clock by then, and she hadn't left Peter's side for an instant. "We'll keep an eye on him if you want to get a cup of coffee," Webster offered, but she shook her head. She had no intention of leaving Peter until things had improved further, no matter how long it took. She hadn't eaten anything since that morning, but she couldn't have eaten at that point if she'd tried.

It was another hour before Peter made another sound, but this time when he did, he said "Mom" again, a little more clearly. "Hurts," he finally added to it in a voice that was barely more than a croak, but he lifted his hand this time, and squeezed hers as much as he could. He was hardly stronger than a baby. They didn't want to give him anything for the pain and risk his slipping back into a coma. "Home," he said finally, while the doctors watched him.

"You want to go home?" Bill Webster asked as Peter looked at him, and ever so slightly, Peter nodded. "Good. We want you to go home too, but you're going to have to talk to me some more before you go anywhere. How do you feel, Peter?" He spoke to his patient far more gently than he had to his patient's mother. But she was grateful now for what they were doing for him.

"Terrible," Peter said in answer to his question. "Hurts."

"What hurts the most?"

"Head."

"Does your neck hurt?" He nodded again and then winced, it obviously pained him to move anything, and with good reason. "Does anything else hurt?"

"No . . . Mommy . . ."

"I'm here, baby. I'm not going anywhere."

"Sorry . . ." he said, looking at her, and she shook her head. He had nothing to be sorry about at this point. "Stupid."

"Yes. Very." The doctor answered for her. "You're lucky you didn't wind up a quadriplegic from something like this." And then he asked him to move his legs and arms, and hands and feet, and Peter did, but he could barely squeeze the doctor's fingers. But Webster and the neurosurgeon were pleased with his progress. And at nine o'clock they told Liz they were moving him to the Trauma ICU to continue to monitor him closely. "I think you can go home and get some rest. He's moving steadily in the right direction. You can come back in the morning."

"Can I sleep here?"

"If you really want to. He should go to sleep

eventually. We might even give him something to make him sleep, if he makes a little more progress. You can use the rest, you've had quite a day here." In spite of himself, he felt sorry for her. As a rule, he tried not to get too involved with his patients, but Liz looked like she'd been through the wringer. "Do you have other kids at home?" he asked, and she nodded. "You might want to go back to them. They must be worried. He was in pretty bad shape when he came in. Did they see it happen?"

"I think so. I'll call and let them know he's better." There had been nothing to say to reassure them until then.

"Why don't you go home for a while? I'll call you if anything happens." Webster sounded firm.

"Will you be here?" She didn't like him, but she was beginning to trust him.

"All night and until noon tomorrow. I promise." He smiled at her, and she was surprised to realize that he was actually decent-looking when he wasn't running roughshod over her, or scowling as he checked the monitors and the chart.

"I hate to leave him," she said honestly.

"It'll do you good, and we'll be busy moving him in a little while. You'll just get in the way here." He had a way with words, and she couldn't help smiling at him. And then she told Peter she'd be back soon, she was going home to the other children.

"I'll be back as fast as I can, I promise," she said to Peter and he smiled.

"Sorry, Mom," he said again. "Really stupid."

"You're really lucky. And I love you. So just hurry up and get better."

"Tell Jamie I'm okay," he said with real effort, but also real progress. It was the longest sentence he'd said since he woke up and started talking to them.

"I will. I'll see you later."

"I'm okay." He was trying to reassure her, which was a good sign. He was cognizant, and not only aware of his surroundings, but the subtler implications of what had happened. She couldn't even bear to think of what it would have been like if he hadn't come out of the coma, or worse, hadn't survived. It didn't bear thinking.

"I expect to see you running up and down the hall when I get back. Okay?" He laughed at her, and she walked slowly out into the hall after she kissed him, and the doctor followed.

"He's a very lucky boy," he said, looking impressed by her. She hadn't faltered for a single moment. "For a while there, I didn't think he was going to come out of it without surgery, and certainly not this quickly. He's young and healthy, and who knows, maybe you made a difference, talking to him like that."

"Whatever it was, thank God he came out of it when he did." Her legs went weak as she thought about it.

"He's going to be here for a couple of weeks, I suspect, so don't wear yourself out all at once. If you want to come back in the morning, he'll be fine."

"I'd rather sleep here. But I'll go home and check on the other children and then come back in a couple of hours."

"How many do you have?" He was curious about her. He didn't know who or what she was, but one thing was obvious to him, she was a wonderful mother and loved her son deeply.

"Five," she answered him. "He's the oldest."

"Leave your number at the desk. I'll call if anything comes up. And if you decide to stay once you get home, don't feel guilty about it. The others may be pretty upset, particularly if they saw it happen. How old is your youngest?"

"Ten. They're ten, eleven, thirteen, and fourteen."

"You've got your hands full."

"They're good kids," she said, and he wanted to say they had a good mother, but he didn't. Instead, he went back to check on Peter again, and she left. It was after nine when she got home, and all the children were still up. The girls were sitting at the kitchen table, crying, and Jamie was sitting on Carole's lap, looking exhausted and pale. They looked like orphans from a war zone, and they jumped at her the minute she walked in the door, trying to read her face, but she was smiling, although she looked worn out and disheveled.

"He's going to be okay. He's got a terrible concussion, and a hairline fracture of a vertebra in his neck, but he's going to be okay now. He's very lucky."

"Can we see him?" They asked as a chorus.

"Not yet," Liz said, as Carole put a plate in front of her with leftover meat loaf from dinner, but Liz couldn't eat a thing.

"When can he come home?" Megan asked, looking anxious.

"Not for a couple of weeks, maybe longer. It depends how fast he recovers." They wanted to know everything, but she spared them the horrors of that afternoon. All they needed to know was that he had survived. They sat together for an hour, and when they went upstairs, Carole told her how sorry she was. She felt entirely responsible for what had happened.

"Don't be silly," Liz said, almost too tired to talk to her, let alone assuage her guilt, but she felt she owed it to her to calm her down. "You can't control everything. They obviously got too rough. He's just damn lucky it didn't kill him, or paralyze him."

"Oh, my God," Carole said, as tears rolled down her cheeks and she blew her nose. "Will he really be all right?"

"They think so. He didn't regain consciousness until a couple of hours ago, but he's talking now. For a while there, I thought . . ." She couldn't even say it, and Carole nodded with tears in her eyes. She had thought the same thing, and the longer it took Liz to come home, and when she didn't call, Carole was certain that the worst was about to happen. They had come damn close though. "I'm going back tonight. I'll go up and pack some things."

"Why don't you sleep here? You look exhausted, Liz, you can use the rest if you're going to be with him tomorrow."

"That's what the doctor said, but I want to be with him tonight. Even at seventeen, this has to be scary for him, and he's in a lot of pain from the concussion."

"Poor kid. What a miserable way to end the summer. Do you think he'll be able to start school in September?"

"We don't know yet." School was the least of

his problems. It had looked so terrifying all afternoon. Liz felt as though she'd been hit by an express train as she thought of it, and she looked as though she had, as Carole's heart went out to her.

Liz walked slowly upstairs, and went in to kiss Jamie good night, but he was already sound asleep, and the girls were in bed. The house seemed strangely quiet without Peter, as she walked into her room and sat down on the bed. She wanted to pack a bag, but suddenly she couldn't move. All she could think of was what had nearly happened, and all she could do was sob with relief. It was after eleven when she finally packed her bag, and midnight when she got back to the hospital to see him. She had delayed for a few minutes to call her mother, who was horrified about Peter's accident when Liz told her. "My God, will he be all right?" she asked in a choked voice, and Liz reassured her and promised that when Peter felt better, he would call her.

Peter was awake when Liz arrived back at the hospital, and continuing to make good progress. He was talking almost normally to one of the nurses when Liz walked into the ICU.

"Hi, Mom," he said the moment he saw her. "How's Jamie?"

"He's fine. Everybody said to tell you they

love you. They wanted to come and see you. I told them to wait awhile, or they'd have been back here with me.''

The nurse set up a bed for her in a corner of the waiting room, and she lay down on it in the tracksuit she'd worn, and she pulled a blanket over her. They had promised to come and wake her if Peter needed her, or got worse again, but they told her they didn't think there would be a problem. His vital signs were good, and he was talking up a storm.

She was just drifting off to sleep when she saw Bill Webster walk into the room, and she sat bolt upright in panic, with her heart pounding as she looked at him. He had changed his green scrubs for gray ones. It was not a particularly attractive costume.

"What happened?"

"Nothing. He's fine. I didn't mean to scare you. I just wanted to see if you needed any-thing . . . something to sleep . . .'' He seemed to hesitate, and she realized how much he cared and she was grateful for what he was doing for Peter, and had already done.

"I'm fine, thank you," she said, unwinding slowly again. "And thank you for everything you've done. I think I'll be able to sleep." She looked so tired, but it didn't really surprise him. It had been an intense afternoon.

"I'm glad he's doing so well." He looked as though he meant it.

"So am I. I'm not sure we'd have lived through it, if he didn't."

"Was your husband ill for a long time?" he asked. For some reason he had assumed it was cancer, but she shook her head.

"He was shot by the husband of one of our clients on Christmas morning." That jogged his memory, and he nodded. He couldn't think of what to say to her, and could only guess what it had been like for her.

"I'm sorry," he said. "I remember seeing it on the news," and then he turned off the light in the waiting room, and left her. It was hard not to admire her. She was still walking around, still reasonable, still coherent, still taking care of her kids and working. He went back to check on Peter then, and smiled as he looked at him. He had been a gift that night to his mother, and she deserved it. Even more than Bill Webster could imagine. But what he knew now was enough. The boy was doing fine. And he smiled to himself as he walked back to his desk to sign some orders. He liked days like this one, days when you won instead of lost. It was one of those days that made him glad he did what he did for a living. For once, the fates had played fair with his patient. He sat back in his chair then, and closed his eyes for a minute. And then he opened them again, and signed the orders they needed from him. He had a long night ahead of him, but he didn't mind. Things had worked out just fine this time, and he was glad.

Chapter 7

Liz slept fitfully for a few hours in the waiting room where Bill Webster had left her, and was back at Peter's bedside before he woke up. And when Peter did wake up he had a tremendous headache, and complained about the brace and the pain at the back of his neck.

Webster came and checked on him at six o'clock in the morning, as he had every hour all through the night. But everything looked fine to him. The neurosurgeon came back later that morning, and seemed pleased with what he saw. He told Liz that her son was a very lucky boy.

She helped the nurses bathe him, and they started him on clear fluids, and in the early afternoon, she went home for a while. The others were still anxious about him, and the girls had a million questions, but as soon as she got home, Liz realized that Jamie was nowhere to be found. She asked Carole about it, who said that she hadn't seen him since breakfast, and when Liz searched the house, she found him sitting quietly in his room.

"Hi, sweetheart, what are you doing up here all by yourself?" She was worried about him, and even more so when he turned to look at her and she could see the devastation on his face. Just seeing him that way made her heart sink like a rock. She went to sit beside him on the floor and took his hand in her own. "Peter said to send you his love. He's going to try and come home soon." But Jamie just shook his head, as two tears rolled slowly down his cheeks into his lap.

"No, he's not. He's gone, like Daddy. I had a dream about him last night."

"Look at me," she said, turning his face gently toward her, and looking straight into his eyes. "I'm not lying to you, Jamie. Peter is going to be fine. He hurt his neck and he has a brace on it, and a big, big headache. But I promise you, he's coming back." There was a long silence between them, as the child searched her eyes.

"Can I see him?" He still looked pretty scary, with tubes everywhere, and monitors flashing and beeping, but she couldn't help wondering if it would be better for Jamie to see him and know for certain that his brother was alive.

"If you really want to. There are a lot of machines around him, they make funny noises, and he has tubes in his arms."

"What kind of tubes?" Jamie looked curious but less frightened.

"Kind of like straws." That was close enough.

"Will they let me see him?" There were no children allowed in the ICU, but she decided to ask Bill Webster, and explain the situation to him. He told her he'd be on duty that evening, and she had promised Peter she'd be back to spend the night.

"I'll ask," she promised, and then gently pulled the child into her arms. "I love you, Jamie. Everything is going to be all right."

"Promise he's not going away like Daddy?"

"I promise," she said, fighting back tears. This was still so hard for all of them, not just for her.

"Pinkie swear?" he asked, holding his little finger up, and she linked it with her own.

"Pinkie swear. I'll ask about your visiting when I see the doctor tonight. Why don't we call Peter this afternoon so you can talk to him?" Jamie's eyes lit up at that.

"Can I?"

"Sure," she promised, and realized that it would be a relief to his sisters too. Jamie came downstairs with her after that, and she rounded up the girls, dialed the hospital, and asked for the Trauma ICU.

They brought a phone to Peter, and he sounded hoarse and weak, but relatively normal in spite of it, he promised to come home as soon as he could, and told his sisters to behave while he was gone. And then he warned Jamie to be careful in the pool, and told him that what he had done was real dumb, and never to do anything like that.

"I miss you guys," he said, sounding like a child again, and Liz could hear tears in his voice, as she listened on the other phone. "I'll come home as soon as I can."

"Mom said she's going to ask if I can come and visit you," Jamie said proudly, and Peter sounded pleased. Liz spoke up then and told Peter she'd be back in a few hours. If he was feeling all right, she wanted to have dinner with the kids.

"That's fine, Mom. Can you bring me something to eat?"

"Like what?" He was still on fluids, and they were talking about starting him on Jell-O that afternoon. He wasn't too excited about that.

"A cheeseburger." His mother laughed at the request.

"You must be feeling a lot better." It was a far cry from the day before when she was begging him to open his eyes and talk to her, as he lay there in another world. "I think you'd better wait a couple of days for that, sweetheart."

"I figured you'd say that." He sounded disappointed.

"I'll see you later."

She went back to the other children then, and Jamie sat on her lap for a while, but he looked less upset than he had been. Talking to Peter had helped. And after he went to play outside, she called her office. According to Jean, there was nothing exciting happening. She had managed to postpone a court appearance, and reschedule some appointments for the following week. But it pointed out to Liz again that everything rested on her shoulders now. There was no one to stand in for her, juggle cases with her, it all depended on her. The children, her work, the catastrophe that had nearly befallen Peter, and the destruction it would have wrought if he had not survived. It was an awesome burden. And she was thinking about it as she drove back to the hospital to see Peter that night.

Bill Webster was back on duty by then, and he smiled when he saw her, but he looked harassed, and only waved as she walked by. It was another hour before he drifted in to the ICU to see Peter, and chat with her.

"How's our star patient doing?"

"He asked for a cheeseburger, I think that's a good sign, don't you?" she asked, as she brushed a lock of red hair out of her eyes. She had been gently rubbing Peter's shoulders for him, and he was still complaining about his massive headache, but they had put him on pain medication, which seemed to help somewhat.

"I think a cheeseburger is an excellent sign. How about tomorrow, Peter?"

"Really?" Peter looked thrilled.

"I think so. We're going to start you on therapy for that neck in a few days, and you might as well get your strength up, if your stomach doesn't object too much." It was good news to Peter, who had hated the Jell-O, and refused to eat it, or the thin clear soup.

Bill Webster checked a few things on Peter's chart, looked carefully at the monitors, and made some notes before he left the ICU again, and Liz followed him out. She wanted to ask him about bringing Jamie to visit the following afternoon.

"I have a favor to ask," she began cautiously, as he listened. He was wearing blue scrubs this time, and he looked as though he hadn't combed his hair in days. But he'd been dealing with a head-on collision all afternoon, three children and five adults had been injured. Two of the children had died that evening. It had been depressing and ugly, and it was a relief, even to him, to see Peter make such good progress. "I know they don't let children visit the ICU," she began, and he nodded, looking only faintly impatient. In his opinion, there were good reasons for not having children in the ICU, they were little germ factories, and his patients were not up to fighting off infections. But Liz was looking at him with a serious expression. "We've all been through a lot in the past year, since their father died," she still hated saying the word, but knew she had to, "and my youngest son is very upset about Peter."

"How old is he?"

"Ten," she hesitated, looking at him, wondering how much she needed to tell him, and then she decided to confide in him. After all, he had saved Peter's life. "He's learning-delayed. He was premature, and suffered a severe oxygen loss, and when they gave him oxygen at the delivery, it caused some damage. This is very hard for him, he saw what happened yesterday, and he thinks Peter may not come back, like his father. It would help a lot if he could see him sometime soon."

There was a long pause as Bill Webster looked at her, and then nodded. She'd been through a lot, he was sure, and so had her kids.

"What can I do to help you?" he asked gently. "You have a lot on your plate, don't you?" The way he said it to her made her eyes fill with tears, and she turned away for a minute to compose herself before she answered. It was just as it had been right after Jack died, when people were kind to her, it broke down her defenses and made her cry.

"Just let him see Peter," she said softly.

"Whenever you like. What about the others? Are they okay about it?" The family had clearly taken a heavy hit when their father was killed, and he wanted to do something now to ease their burdens. It made him realize what their brother represented to them, and to their mother. It gave him some insight into what he'd seen between them the day before.

"I think the girls understand, but it would reassure them to see him. I just didn't want to push too far. But it's really important for Jamie."

"Bring him in first thing tomorrow."

"Thank you," she said, feeling moved by what he'd said to her, and not sure how to thank him.

She went back to Peter then, and stayed with him until he fell asleep, and then she went back to sleep herself on the couch in the waiting room. It was dark in the room, but she was still awake when Bill opened the door and looked in at her. He couldn't see if she was sleeping, and he was afraid to disturb her. He just stood watching her for a long moment until he spoke.

"Liz?" It was the first time he had used her first name, and she sat up, worried about Peter again.

"Is something wrong?" She set her feet down on the carpet, and tossed off the blanket she'd been given by the nurses.

"No, everything's fine. I'm sorry. I didn't mean to scare you. I just wanted to see if you were all right. . . . I wondered if you wanted a cup of tea or something." It was the middle of the night and coffee didn't seem like an appropriate suggestion. He was working, but she was supposed to be asleep. "Did I wake you?" he asked in the dark, feeling guilty for disturbing her. But he'd been thinking about her and wanted to talk.

"No, I was awake. My sleep habits aren't what they used to be, before . . ." The words drifted off, but they both understood. "Maybe some tea would help, or soup or something." There was a machine down the hall, near his office. She'd bought both soup and tea there before, but as she put her shoes on and followed him down the hall, he offered her tea from a pot in his office.

She sat down in a chair, feeling rumpled and uncombed, but he didn't look like he'd care. He looked worse than she did, after working all night.

"What kind of law do you specialize in?" he asked, as he sipped a mug of coffee.

"Family law . . . divorce. . . ."

He nodded knowingly. "I've had a little experience with that myself, but not in a long time." He didn't look as though the memory was pleasant, but he managed a small, wintry smile.

"Are you divorced?" she asked, and he nodded. "Kids?"

"Nope. No time. I was a resident when we got married, and she was an intern. Some people manage to have kids then, but it always seemed foolish to me. I didn't want to have kids until I could spend some time with them, and enjoy them. You know," he smiled, "like maybe when I'm eighty." He had a nice smile, and a kinder look in his eyes than she had at first suspected. She had disliked him intensely when she first met him. He seemed so brusque, so rude, so uncaring, but she realized now that he had more important things on his mind, like saving lives, and sometimes, in his line of work, it was a matter of split seconds, and getting information from patients' families as fast as you could. The day before he had seemed so harsh and abrupt to her, and now he seemed both pleasant and kind. "I've been divorced for ten years," he told her then, volunteering more information than she'd asked for, but she was that kind of person. Her clients always told her more than she needed to know too, but sometimes that was helpful. And she found she wanted to know more about him.

"With no desire to remarry?" she asked with interest.

"Very little. And no time. I think the first time cured me. Our divorce was pretty bitter. She had an affair with my chief resident, which didn't actually sit well with me. Everybody in the hospital knew it before I did, and felt sorry for me. They got married eventually and have three kids. She gave up medicine during her residency, it was just a hobby for her. We were very different." To say the least.

"My husband and I practiced law together for eighteen years, we had a good time together. It's nice being in the same line of work," Liz said quietly, trying not to think of him too much. She was tired, and emotional, and she knew she would cry easily if Bill asked the right questions about Jack. "To be honest, he liked family law more than I did. I always liked the philanthropic stuff, and hopeless causes, fighting for the rights of the underdog. But he had a good sense of where the money was, and he was right, we had five kids to think of."

"And now? You're still doing divorce work?" She nodded. "Why? You could do anything you want."

"Not exactly," she smiled. "I still have the same five kids, their feet are bigger, and their shoes are more expensive than ever. So is their education. One of these days I'll have four in college. Jack was right. Family law is very lucrative, even if it gets me down sometimes. In divorce work, you see people at their worst. The nicest people turn into monsters when they're mad at their spouses. But I feel I owe it to my husband to keep our practice going. He worked hard building it, I can't just walk away now." From that, or their kids, or their house, or their responsibilities, it was all hers now, and Bill got that.

"Do you ever think about doing a different kind of law?" he asked, intrigued by her. She was smart, and nice, and very pretty. There was a softness to her which appealed to him, and a love for her son that touched his heart.

"Sometimes I think about doing something else," she answered him, "but not very often. Do you?" She turned the question on him, and he poured some more coffee into his mug and shook his head.

"Never. I love this. It's about as high pressure as it gets, you have to make split-second decisions, and they have to be the right ones. The stakes are high, and there's no room for mistakes. It forces me to be the best I can be all the time. I like that."

"It sounds like climbing Everest every day, and it must be heartbreaking sometimes." She was thinking of Peter the day before and how easily they might have lost him. And the two children he had lost that night.

"It's heartbreaking too often," Bill answered. "I hate losing."

"So did Jack," she smiled. "I'm not too crazy about it myself, but for him it was a personal affront if he lost a single motion. He had to win every time, which is probably what cost him his life. He played hardball with a man who went berserk over it. I was afraid of it. . . . I warned him . . . but he didn't believe me. I guess no one could really have predicted what happened. It was an insane thing for our client's husband to have done. But he was insane. He killed his wife, and then my husband, and then shot himself in our office." Just saying it reminded her of the grisly scene again and she closed her eyes for a second, as Bill watched her.

"It must have been a nightmare for you and the kids," he said, sorry for her.

"It still is sometimes. It's going to take us a long time to get over it, but we're doing better. We were married for nineteen years, you don't forget all that in a few months, we were very happy for a long time."

"You were lucky," he said quietly. He had

never felt that way about anyone, not even the woman he'd married, or the two he lived with after her. And in the years since, he had given up his search for the perfect woman. Women drifted in and out of his life from time to time, and he never got too attached to them anymore. It seemed safer that way, and simpler. He didn't need or want more than that.

"We were very lucky," Liz echoed, and then stood up finally and thanked him for the tea. "I guess I'd better try to get some sleep before Peter wakes up. I was going to try and go to the office in the morning, and come back in the afternoon with Jamie."

"I'll be here." Bill smiled at her, and reminded her that he wanted to meet Jamie when he came in.

She turned in the doorway then, and looked at him, with a look of sorrow in her eyes. As she had said to him, for her, the nightmare of losing Jack was not yet over. "Thanks for letting me talk. It helps sometimes."

"Anytime, Liz." But he hadn't done it entirely for her. He liked talking to her, liked the boy. He was just sorry they'd had so much trouble, so much pain.

She went back to the couch in the waiting room then, and lay awake for a long time. She was thinking about him and the lonely, demanding life he led. It didn't seem like much of a life to her, but these days hers wasn't much of a life either, except for her work and her kids. She fell asleep finally, dreaming about Jack, and he seemed to be saying something to her. He was pointing at something and trying to warn her, and when she turned, she saw Peter diving neatly off a high diving board, into concrete. She awoke with a feeling of panic, mixed in with the old familiar sadness again. There was always that terrible moment when she woke up when she remembered that something horrible had happened. And then in an instant, she would remember that Jack had died. She still hated waking up in the morning. It was what made it so hard to go to sleep at night, knowing she'd have to wake up and face the sharp blow of reality all over again.

She had combed her hair and washed her face and brushed her teeth, but she still felt rumpled and messy. Peter was awake when she went back to the ICU in the morning. And he was complaining about the fact that he was hungry and no one would feed him. Eventually, they gave him a bowl of oatmeal, and he made a terrible face as his mother fed it to him.

"Yerghkkkk!" he said, looking five instead of seventeen. "That's disgusting."

"Be a good boy, and eat it. It's good for you," she scolded him, but he clenched his teeth and pursed his lips, and when she set the spoon down, she was laughing. "What did you have in mind instead?"

"I want waffles." He was referring to hers, and she had purposely never made them again, since the morning Jack died. She just couldn't. And the children understood. Although they were a family favorite, none of the children had ever asked her to make them. But this time, Peter had forgotten. "And bacon," he added. "I hate oatmeal."

"I know you do. Maybe they'll start feeding you real food today. I'll talk to Dr. Webster."

"I think he likes you." Peter smiled at his mother.

"I like him too. He saved your life. That's a good way to impress me."

"I mean, *he likes you*. I saw him watching you yesterday."

"I think you're hallucinating, but you're cute anyway, even if you won't eat your breakfast."

"What if he asks you out, would you go?" Peter asked the question with a grin.

"Don't be ridiculous. He's your doctor, not some high school Romeo. I think the bump on your head jiggled your brain." She was amused, but not particularly interested in what he was saying. Bill Webster was a nice man, and they'd had a nice talk the night before, but it meant nothing to either of them.

"Would you, Mom?" Peter was persistent, and she only laughed at him, refusing to address the question seriously. There was no need to. What he was saying was absurd.

"No, I wouldn't. I'm not interested in going out with anyone. And he's not interested in going out with me. So you can stop matchmaking, and concentrate on getting better."

She helped the nurses bathe him then, and later that morning, she went to her office. Jean had put out as many fires as she could, and fortunately things weren't as busy as they could be. It was the middle of August, and most people were on vacation till after Labor Day.

She went home that afternoon to see the kids, and have dinner with them. She spoke to Peter on the phone several times that afternoon, and he was in good spirits. A number of his friends had come by to see him, and they'd brought him something to eat. He and Jessica had broken up in June, so there was no current girlfriend in his life to fuss over him, but he was just happy to see his friends. And Liz finally had a few minutes to call Victoria and her mother too. She'd told them both about the accident after it happened, and it was nice to be able to reassure both of them. As usual, her mother made ominous predictions about possible unexpected lethal aftereffects, and Victoria asked her what she could do to help. But there was nothing anyone could do yet. It was just nice for Liz to hear her voice and unwind a little bit. And after the brief respite, she went back to the work on her desk.

After dinner at home that night, Liz took a shower and changed, and told Jamie to put his shoes on. She was taking him to see his brother. She had asked the girls to wait one more day, because she knew that the onslaught of their talk and laughter and questions and well-intentioned fussing over Peter would exhaust him. But Jamie's visit was as much for Jamie as for Peter. She knew he still needed to see that Peter was okay.

Jamie was quiet on the way to the hospital, and she thought he looked a little anxious as he stared out the window. And then finally he turned to her as they pulled into the hospital parking lot and asked her a pointed question.

"Will it scare me, Mommy?" It was honest, and what he asked her touched her, and she was honest with him.

"Maybe a little. Hospitals are a little scary. It's a lot of people and machines and funny sounds.

But Peter doesn't look scary." His face was a little bruised, but not very. "He has a funny-looking collar on, and he's in a big bed that goes up and down if you push a button."

"Will he ever come home again?"

"Yes, baby, very soon. Before school starts."

"Is that soon?" Jamie wasn't good about time, and he knew it.

"In a couple of weeks," she explained to him. "Maybe even sooner. There's a nice doctor there who wants to meet you. His name is Bill."

"Will he give me a shot?" Jamie looked panicked. For him, this was not only an adventure, it was an ordeal, but he was willing to walk through fire to see Peter, or do whatever he had to do.

"No, he won't give you a shot," his mother said gently.

"Good. I hate shots. Did he give Peter a shot?" He was worried about his brother.

"A bunch of them, but Peter's a big boy and doesn't mind." The only thing he hated was Jell-O and oatmeal. His friends had brought him a pizza that afternoon, and he had sounded happy when he told her. "Shall we go in now?" Jamie nodded and slipped a hand into hers as they walked into the main lobby. He held her hand tightly in his own, and she could feel that his palm was damp, as they went up in the elevator to the Trauma ICU, and he flinched visibly as they got out of the elevator and saw someone on a gurney.

"Is he dead?" Jamie asked in a horrified whisper, standing close to her. The man's eyes were closed and there was a nurse standing next to him.

"He's just sleeping, Jamie, it's okay. Nothing bad is going to happen." She shepherded him quickly down the hall to the ICU, and they could see Peter the minute they walked in. He was sitting up in bed, and he gave a whoop of glee when he saw Jamie. And the minute Jamie saw him, he smiled from ear to ear.

"Hi, big guy, come over here and kiss me!" he shouted, and Jamie ran to him and then came to a dead stop when he saw all the monitors and machines. He was afraid to get too near. "Come on," Peter encouraged him, "just one more big step, and I've got you." Jamie took the last step as though he were fording a stream filled with snakes, but as soon as he could, Peter grabbed him firmly, and pulled him closer. He was smiling at him, and leaned over to give him a hug and a kiss, and as Liz approached she saw that Jamie was beaming. "Boy, I missed you!"

"I missed you too. I thought you were dead," Jamie said simply, "but Mom said you weren't. I didn't believe her at first, that's why she brought me here to see you."

"You bet I'm not dead. But it was a dumb thing to do, jumping into the pool like that. You'd better not do anything as stupid as I did, or you'll be in big trouble with me, kiddo. How's everything at home?"

"Boring. The girls keep telling everyone what happened to you. They all cried when you went away in the ambulance. Me too," he said, looking up at his big brother in relief. This was just what he needed. "Can I make your bed go up and down?" he asked with interest, as he looked around. There were other people in the ICU, but their curtains were drawn, and he couldn't see them.

"Sure." Peter showed him the buttons and how to do it, and he winced as Jamie first flung him up then down, and then moved him to a sitting position.

"Does that hurt?" Jamie was fascinated with making the bed move.

"A little," Peter admitted.

"Do you want to lie down again?"

"Okay, I'll tell you how far, and when to stop." Peter was always a good sport about making Jamie happy. And as Jamie was concentrating on flattening the bed out again, Bill Webster walked in, and looked at the scene with interest.

He glanced at Liz, and then back at her two sons. Peter had just told him to let go of the button, and Jamie was satisfied that he had done a good job of it. He wanted to do it again, but this time Peter asked him not to. He was still in more pain than he wanted to admit.

"Hi, Doc," Peter said as he looked up, and Jamie glanced at Bill with a look of suspicion.

"Are you going to bed?" Jamie asked politely, staring at the green scrubs he was wearing.

"No. I get to wear these to work, isn't that silly? That way, I can fall asleep anytime I want." He was teasing, but Jamie looked up at him with big, serious brown eyes. Despite Jamie's dark brown hair, and Peter's red, there was a striking resemblance between them. "Introduce me to your brother," he said to Peter, who duly introduced Jamie to the doctor.

"I don't want a shot," Jamie explained, so there would be no misunderstanding between them from the first.

"Neither do I," he said, keeping a respectful distance, not wanting to upset the boy. He knew of his limitations from his mother. "I'll promise not to give you one, if you don't give me one either." Jamie laughed as Bill said it.

"I promise," Jamie said solemnly. And then for no particular reason, he volunteered a piece of information about himself, as though he thought some kind of social exchange was expected of him. "I won three medals at the Special Olympics. Mom coached me."

"What did you compete in?" Bill asked with a look of profound interest.

"Running long jump, hundred yard dash, and sack race." He reeled them off with pride, and Liz smiled as she watched him.

"Your mom must be a pretty good coach if you won all that."

"She is. I only won fourth place with my dad. He shouted a lot more than Mom did. But Mom made me work harder and stay out later while we trained."

"Persistence wins the prize," Bill said more to Liz than to Jamie and she smiled at him, slightly embarrassed to have Jamie extolling her virtues. "That must have been pretty exciting."

"It was," Jamie said, smiling, and then turned back to his brother and asked if he could work the bed again. And although Peter didn't look too happy about it, he let Jamie do it, as Bill and Liz stepped outside for a moment to talk.

"How's he doing?" Liz asked. Peter still looked very tired to her, and she could see that his head and neck were hurting.

"He's doing fine," Bill reassured her, "he's

my star patient. Your younger son is a great kid, you must be proud of him," he said, glancing at Jamie through the windows of the ICU.

"I am." And then she smiled at Bill. "Thank you for letting me bring him. He was panicked about Peter. This really reassured him. He hasn't looked this happy in two days."

"He can come back anytime, as long as he doesn't give me a shot." Bill smiled at her and she laughed as they wandered back into the ICU, and Liz rescued Peter from Jamie, who was wreaking havoc with the bed.

"I think it's time to go home, gentlemen. Peter needs to get some rest, and so do you." She looked at Jamie solemnly. "The doctor says you can come back soon."

"Next time, bring a pizza," Peter added, and kissed Jamie good-bye a few minutes later. Jamie waved from the door of the ICU, and then walked back to the elevator with his mother. They were still standing there when Bill saw them, and came over to thank Jamie for coming.

"I liked it. It was cool. I thought it would scare me," Jamie said honestly, which was part of his charm. He always said what was on his mind. "The ambulance made a lot of noise when it took Peter away," Jamie informed him, and Bill nodded.

"Ambulances do that. But it's usually pretty

quiet here. Come back and visit again." He smiled at him, and Jamie nodded.

"My sisters are coming tomorrow. They talk a lot, they might make Peter tired." Bill laughed out loud at that, and didn't dare add that sometimes women did that. He didn't know Liz well enough to say it, and wasn't sure yet of her sense of humor, but he was amused by the comment Jamie had made.

"I'll make sure they don't wear him out. Thanks for telling me." The elevator arrived then, and Jamie waved as the doors closed. Bill had already asked her if she'd be back that night, but she had decided to spend the night at home with her children, and come back in the morning to see Peter again. And she had thanked Bill again for making Jamie's visit so easy and so successful. He was very pleased with it as they drove back to Tiburon and he said so.

"I like Peter's bed, and the doctor. He's nice. And he hates shots too," he reminded his mother. "I think Peter likes him."

"We all do," Liz agreed. "He saved your brother's life."

"Then I like him too." He told his sisters all about his visit to Peter and about the bed that went up and down, and the doctor who hated shots and had saved Peter's life. It had been a big adventure for him. He slept in his mother's bed that night, but he slept peacefully, and didn't have nightmares. Unlike his mother, who dreamed endlessly about Jack, and Peter's accident, and Bill, and Jamie and the girls. It was a night filled with anxieties and accidents and people. And she felt as though she'd ridden in a rodeo all night when she awoke the next morning.

"Are you tired, Mommy?" Jamie asked when he woke her up at six.

"Very," she said with a groan. The past few days had taken a toll on her. The terror of nearly losing her son made her feel as though she had been beaten, and she had been. It was like a small replay of what she had gone through when she lost Jack, but at least this time, it had a happy ending.

She made breakfast for the kids, left for work, appeared in court, and went back to the hospital to meet Carole and the girls. Jamie stayed with a neighbor because Liz didn't want him to overdo it, and it was the girls' turn. They laughed and talked and cried, and checked out everything, gave him the news, told him about their romances and friends, and told him how happy they were that he was okay. But Jamie had been right, Liz realized. Peter was exhausted when they left an hour later, and needed a shot of pain medication. And when he was finally asleep, Bill and Liz stood in the waiting room to talk.

"Jamie was right," she said, looking worried, "the girls wiped him out."

"Girls have a way of doing that," he smiled, "but I think it was good for him, a little taste of real life to balance the ICU. He needs that." They talked about when he could go home then, and Bill thought they could count on his being home by Labor Day, less than two weeks away. He just wanted to be sure all the swelling had gone down in his brain, so there wouldn't be complications, and that sounded sensible to her. But it reminded her of something she wanted to discuss with the children. Their annual Labor Day party. They hadn't been planning to give it this year, but after what had happened, and the tragedy they'd been spared, she thought it was time for a celebration. And going back to Lake Tahoe was now impossible. It was too much for Peter to travel so soon.

"Can he go back to school on schedule?" she asked, looking concerned.

"Close enough. Maybe a week late. Nothing too dramatic. He can't drive though." And Liz had been planning to take him on a college tour in September. That would have to wait awhile too, until he was stronger.

They talked about the details of his recovery for a while, and he invited her back to his office for a cup of coffee before she left, and she sank into a chair looking exhausted.

"Long day?" he asked, looking sympathetic. She had so much responsibility, he knew, and he was impressed by how well she handled it, how calm she was, and how loving she was with her children.

"No longer than yours," she said kindly.

"I don't have five kids, and one in the hospital." Or a child who was learning-delayed, and obviously needed more careful attention than the others, not to mention three adolescent daughters, who were clamoring for her attention. "When I think about it, I don't know how you do it."

"Neither do I sometimes. You just do what you have to."

"And you?" he asked quietly, looking at her over his coffee mug. "Who takes care of you, Liz?"

"I do. Peter sometimes. My secretary, my housekeeper, my friends. I'm pretty lucky." It was an odd way to look at it, from his perspective. After losing her husband whom she counted on for twenty years. She was trying to do it all on her own. He admired her a lot for what she was doing, and it was obvious to him she did it well.

"When I look at you, I feel guilty for how little responsibility I have. I don't even have a goldfish. Just myself. I guess I'm pretty selfish."

Compared to her, he felt as though he had very little to deal with.

"Just different. Everyone has different needs, Bill. You obviously know yours, and you have it the way you want it." He was old enough to have done something about it, if he didn't. He was forty-five years old, he had said a few days before, and his life obviously suited him, just as hers did. "I'd be lost without my kids."

"I can see why. They're all terrific. And that doesn't just happen. You put a lot into it, and it shows." He remembered what Jamie had said about her coaching him for the Olympics. He couldn't help wondering when she found the time.

"They're worth it, and they make me happy. Speaking of which," she said, putting down her mug and standing up, "I'd better get home before they disown me. I'll see you tomorrow."

"I'm off for a few days, but Peter will be in good hands." He gave her the doctor's name, and told her when he'd be back. He was going up to Mendocino.

"Have fun," she said, smiling at him, "you've earned it."

And that night when she went home, she talked to the kids about the Labor Day party, and she was surprised to find they had mixed emotions about it. Megan and Jamie thought it was a great idea, but Rachel and Annie thought it was a betrayal of their father to have it without him. It had been their father's favorite holiday, other than the Fourth of July.

"Who'll do the barbecue?" Rachel asked plaintively.

"We will," Liz said calmly. "We do barbecues all the time. Peter can help. I just think we need to celebrate the fact that he's okay, and still with us." And when she put it that way, they grudgingly accepted. By the end of the week, they were actually excited about it. They were all going to invite friends, and so was Liz. They had about sixty names on the list, and Liz was looking forward to it. It was the first time she had entertained since Jack died, but it had been eight months and seemed respectable. And Peter was thrilled when they told him about it.

And by the time he was ready to come home, four days before Labor Day, more than fifty people had accepted. She was working out Peter's discharge plan and his therapy schedule with Bill Webster, when she thought of extending an invitation to him. "It's kind of a celebration for Peter," she explained, "it would be great if you could come. It's very informal, just jeans and sweaters."

"Can I wear scrubs? I don't think I own any-

thing else. I never have time to go anywhere."
But he looked pleased to be invited, and told her
that if he wasn't working, he'd be there.

"We'd love to have you." They had a lot to
thank him for, and it was a nice way to do it. She
had sent him a case of wine too, and he'd been
pleased to receive it from her. But suddenly it
seemed right that he be there to celebrate Peter's
homecoming. Without him, Peter might not have
been there at all, it was an intolerable thought.

Most of all, Bill urged her not to let Peter
overdo it. He was young, and he'd be straining at
the bit once he got home, wanting to see his
friends and run around with them. But other-
wise, Bill thought he'd be fine, and have no
residual effect of the accident, once he finished
his therapy, which would be by Christmas. "Keep
a tight rein on him for a while," he admonished
her, and she nodded.

"I'll do that." He wasn't going to be able to
drive for a month or two, until he got the brace
off his neck, and she knew that that was really
going to be hard on Peter, and she'd be playing
chauffeur more than she had time for. But someone had to do it, and a lot of the time, Carole was
busy with the girls and Jamie. "We'll manage."

"Keep in touch. And call me if he has any
problems."

On the morning Peter left the hospital, Bill

came to say good-bye to both of them, and he shook Liz's hand with a warm look. It was obvious that he was going to miss her. She had spent a fair amount of time in his office, drinking coffee and chatting, and they had grown comfortable with each other. She reminded him about the Labor Day party, and he said he'd do his best to be there.

"He'll be there, Mom," Peter confirmed as they drove away.

"Not if he has to work," she said matter-of-factly, but she was sorry to see the last of him too. After the experience he'd gotten them through, he felt like a friend now, and she would be forever grateful to him.

"He'll be there," Peter repeated smugly. "I told you, he likes you."

"Don't be such a wiseass," she said with a grin, unconcerned by what he was saying. He was just Peter's doctor.

"I'll bet you ten bucks he comes," Peter said, readjusting his neck brace.

"You can't afford it," his mother said, and slipped quietly into the traffic. And whether or not Bill came to their Labor Day party, she assured herself, was entirely unimportant. She had convinced herself of it, though not Peter, as he smiled at her.

"I remember you. You don't like shots either." Jamie grinned up at him.

"Right. How's Peter doing?"

"Pretty good, except he yells at me when I jump on him."

"He's right, not to yell, but you need to be a little careful with him. His neck is kind of broken."

"I know. That's why he wears the big necklace."

"I guess you could call it that. Where's your mom?" Bill asked, smiling.

"Over there." He pointed to the barbecue, and Bill nodded, watching her make hamburgers. She was wearing a barbecue apron over jeans, and her red hair stuck out in the crowd, as did Peter's. And in spite of the fact that she was hard at work, she was smiling, and looked very pretty. Her hair had grown over the summer, and she was wearing it long on her shoulders. And as though sensing Bill watching her, she looked up, and saw him. She waved a spatula toward him, and he approached slowly, followed by Jamie. And when he got there, Bill saw that Peter was standing near her, wearing what Jamie called his "necklace."

"How's it going?" the doctor asked his patient, and Peter grinned, and spoke to his mother in an undertone, pretending to hand her something.

"You owe me ten bucks, Mom."

"He came to see you," she whispered sotto voce, and then turned to greet Bill and offer him a glass of wine. He smiled at her, and asked for a Coke instead, since he was on call. The mood around them was casual and festive.

"You look very professional with that barbecue." Bill smiled at her and sipped his Coke.

"I learned from an expert."

"Peter seems to be doing fine," he said, casting a glance at his patient. Peter was having fun with his friends, and flipping hamburgers, despite the cumbersome neck brace.

"He wants to go back to school next week," she said, looking worried for a minute.

"If you think he's up to it, let him. I trust your judgment."

"Thank you." She turned the barbecue over to Carole and Peter then, and one of their neighbors lent a hand, so she could walk off with Bill for a few minutes. They sat down on two empty chairs and she sipped a Coke. She wasn't much of a drinker. "How are things at the hospital?" It seemed funny being here with him, away from the concerns they had shared about Peter. Now they were on their own, like two ordinary people, and she felt suddenly shy with him.

"Things at the hospital are too busy. And they'll get worse before they get better this weekend. Holiday weekends are killers, literally. Car accidents, gunshot wounds, attempted suicides. It's amazing what people can come up with when they're off work for a few days, especially when you put a steering wheel in their hands.''

"It's nice that you could get off and take the time to come over."

"I didn't. I'm on call. I've got my pager on, but I figured they could live without me for a while. I left my chief resident in charge. He's good, he won't call me unless he has to. What about you, Liz? How are the holidays for you? They can't be easy."

"This one is better than I expected. The first of everything has been rough. Valentine's Day, Easter, the kids' birthdays, Fourth of July, but Labor Day is kind of innocuous. I thought this would be fun for the children." And everyone seemed to be having a good time, especially her children. They looked happy to have their friends around, it was the first time the family had entertained since Christmas.

"I used to love holidays when I was a kid. Now they're just workdays." His life sounded lonely to her, but he seemed to like it that way. She had noticed that he was at the hospital constantly when Peter was there, which made it even nicer that he had come to her party. "What do you do with your spare time when you're not working and chasing kids?'' He looked at her with interest as he asked the question and she laughed as she answered.

''What else is there? You mean there's life after work and kids? I'm not sure I remember what that feels like.''

''Maybe you need to be reminded,'' he said casually. ''When was the last time you went to the movies?''

''Hmm . . .'' She thought about it and shook her head. It was hard to believe it had been as long as it had been. She had dropped kids off and picked them up at the movie house in Mill Valley, but she hadn't gone herself in months. ''I think the last time I went to the movies was last Thanksgiving.'' With Jack of course. They had gone, as they always did, after everyone had settled down after Thanksgiving dinner. It had been a tradition with them.

''Maybe we could go to a movie sometime,'' he said hopefully, as his pager went off, and he looked down at his belt where he had clipped it. The display told him it was an emergency, and he took a cellular phone out of his pocket and called the hospital. He listened carefully, told them what to do, and then turned to Liz with a look of disappointment. ''They've got a nasty one on their hands, Liz. A couple of kids in a head-on. I'd better get back. I was hoping for a hamburger and a little more time. You'll have to give me a rain check."

"How about taking a hamburger with you?" she asked as she walked him toward the gate to the backyard. The barbecue was set up right near it, and she asked Peter to wrap one up in some tinfoil, and handed it to Bill as she walked him to his car. It was a ten-year-old Mercedes. He had a certain style about him, although it was hard to tell as he wandered around the hospital in scrubs and clogs. But here he was wearing immaculate, pressed jeans, and well-polished loafers, and his hair was impeccably combed, which it hadn't been any of the other times she'd seen him.

"Thanks for the hamburger," he smiled. "I'll call you for that movie. Maybe next week?"

"I'd like that," she said, feeling shy again, and suddenly very young. It had been years since a man had invited her to the movies. But what the hell, he was nice, and respectable, and he was right, she needed to get out more than she had been.

Victoria commented on Bill's brief appearance when Liz stopped for a minute to talk to her after he left.

"He's cute," Victoria said with a mischievous smile, "and he likes you."

"That's what Peter says." Liz grinned, and

then looked serious again. "He's great at what he does."

"Did he ask you out?" her friend asked bluntly, sounding hopeful.

"Don't be silly, Vic. We're just friends." But the truth was, he had, although Liz was surprised to realize she didn't want to admit it to her. It didn't mean anything. Just a movie. And maybe they'd never do it after all. Liz told herself it wasn't worth mentioning to Victoria, and then moved on to check on her other guests.

The party went on for hours, and it was after eleven when the last guests went home. The food had been good, the wine plentiful, and the people pleasant and happy. They'd all had a good time, and as the kids helped her clean up and carry the stray glasses inside, she was glad she had done it. She was helping Carole load the dishwasher when the phone rang, and she glanced at the clock in surprise, it was after midnight, and she couldn't imagine who would call them.

She answered it, wondering if one of the guests had forgotten something, and was surprised to hear a familiar voice. It was Bill, calling to thank her for the party.

"I thought you'd probably still be up. Has everyone left?"

"Just a few minutes ago. Your timing is perfect. How did your emergency go?"

He sighed before he answered, he didn't like talking about it. Some situations were better than others. "We lost one of the kids, but the other one is doing fine. It happens that way sometimes." But he sounded as though he took it to heart each time he lost one.

"I don't know how you do it," she said softly.

"It's what I do." And it was obvious that he loved it, particularly when he made a difference, as he did much of the time. "So when are we going to the movies?" He didn't even give her time to answer or reconsider. "How about tomorrow? I have a night off, and I'm not on call, a rarity, believe me. We'd better grab it while we can. What about pizza and a movie?"

"Best offer I've had all night . . . all year," she smiled. "Sounds good to me."

"Me too. I'll pick you up at seven."

"I'll see you then, Bill. And thank you. I hope it's a peaceful night there."

"And for you too," he said gently. He remembered how much trouble she had sleeping.

She was still smiling to herself when she hung up the phone, and Peter walked into the kitchen. He looked at her, and then raised an eyebrow as he asked a question.

"And who was that?"

"No one important," she said vaguely. But Peter was staring at her with a look of concentration. He didn't believe her, and then suddenly he knew, and grinned as he teased her.

"It was Bill Webster, wasn't it, Mom? Tell the truth. It was . . . right?"

"Yeah. Maybe." She looked faintly sheepish.

"I told you he likes you! That's terrific."

"What's terrific?" Megan asked as she joined them in the kitchen. Carole was through loading the dishwasher by then, and the younger children had gone to bed a few minutes after the guests left.

"My doctor likes Mom," Peter said with obvious pleasure. He liked him.

"What doctor?" Megan looked surprised at what her brother had just said.

"The one who saved my life, dummy. Who else?"

"What do you mean, 'He likes Mom.' What's that supposed to mean?"

"It means he called her."

"For a *date*?" She looked horrified as she glanced from Peter to her mother, and Peter fired another question at her.

"I don't know. Did he ask you for a date, Mom?" He looked vastly amused, but Megan didn't.

"Sort of," she admitted, and Megan looked outraged. "We're going to the movies tomorrow." There was no point hiding it from them, they'd see him pick her up anyway. And besides, she had nothing to hide. He was a nice guy, and Peter's doctor. They were just friends, and she was sure he had nothing more lurid in mind than what he had proposed, pizza and a movie. "It's no big deal. I just thought it might be fun," she said apologetically, as Megan continued to glare at her.

"That's disgusting. What about Daddy?"

"What about Daddy?" Peter pointedly asked his sister. "He's gone. Mom isn't. She can't sit here taking care of us forever."

"Why not?" Megan didn't see his point, and what she did see of it, she didn't like. In her opinion, her mother had no reason to be dating. "Mom doesn't need to go out," she said both to Peter and her mother. "She has us."

"That *is* the point exactly. She needs more than that in her life. After all, she had Daddy," Peter said, sounding firm.

"That's different," Megan said stubbornly.

"No, it isn't," Peter insisted, as their mother stayed out of it, but she was fascinated by the conflict of opinions. Megan was adamant that she shouldn't be dating, and Peter was clear that she needed more in her life than just work and children, which was precisely why Bill Webster had invited her out. He had said much the same thing as Peter. But it was equally obvious that Megan felt threatened by the idea of a man in her mother's life who wasn't her father.

"What do you think Daddy would say about your going out, Mom?" she asked her mother directly.

"I think he'd say it's about time," Peter said simply. "It's been nearly nine months, and she has a right. Hell, when Andy Martin's mom died last year, his father got remarried in five months. Mom hasn't even looked at another man since Dad died," Peter said fairly, but Megan looked even more worried.

"Are you going to *marry* the doctor?"

"No, Megan," Liz said quietly, "I'm not going to marry anyone. I'm going to eat pizza and see a movie. It's pretty harmless." But it was interesting to her to realize the strong reaction her children had to it, both pro and con. It made her think about it herself as she walked slowly upstairs to her bedroom. Was it wrong? Was it a crazy thing to do, or inappropriate? Was it too soon to be "dating"? But she wasn't dating Bill, they were just going out for movies and dinner, and she certainly didn't want to marry anyone, as Megan had accused. She couldn't imagine marrying anyone after Jack. He had been the perfect husband for her, and anyone else would fall short, she was sure. This was just an evening out, and Bill was just a friend. But Megan was still on the warpath when Bill came to pick her mother up the next evening promptly at seven. Megan glared at him, and stomped up the stairs as loudly as she dared after she let him in. She didn't say a word to him, or introduce herself, and Liz apologized for her being so rude, but Jamie made up for it as he came downstairs with a broad smile to greet Bill. He was happy to see him. And Bill smiled and chatted with him before they left for dinner.

"Did you have fun at the party last night?" Bill stroked the silky dark hair as he asked him.

"It was fun." Jamie nodded. "I ate too many hot dogs and got a stomachache. But it was fun before that."

"I thought so too," Bill agreed, and then pretended to look worried. "You're not going to give me a shot, are you, Jamie?" The child laughed at the joke, and then Bill asked him if he'd ever flown a kite, and Jamie admitted that he hadn't. "You'll have to come fly mine with me sometime," he said pleasantly. "I have a really great one. It's an old-fashioned box kite I made myself, and it flies really well. We'll take it out to the beach sometime and fly it."

"I'd like that," Jamie said with wide eyes and a look of interest.

Rachel and Annie came down to say hi to him then, but Megan never appeared again. She was sulking in her room, and furious with her mother. Peter was out, he'd been picked up by friends since he couldn't drive, and Bill said to say hello to him as they left. Jamie promised to tell Peter when he got back.

"They're great kids," he said admiringly. "I don't know how you do it."

"Easy," she smiled as she got into his comfortable Mercedes, "I just love them a lot."

"You make it sound a lot easier than it is. I just can't see myself doing that," he said, as though contemplating a liver transplant, or open-heart surgery. He made it sound painful and difficult, and potentially fatal. Being a parent had always been something of a mystery to him.

"Can't see yourself doing what?" she asked, as he started the car and backed down her driveway.

"Being married and having kids. You make it look so effortless, but I know damn well it isn't. You have to be good at it. It's an art form. It's a lot tougher than practicing medicine, from all I know."

"You learn it as you go along. They teach you."

"It's not as simple as that, Liz, and you know it. Most kids act like juvenile delinquents, and wind up on drugs, or something close to it.

199

You're damn lucky to have five kids like that," and he included Jamie in the compliment just as she did. He was a terrific kid, and despite his challenges, he only took a little more care and attention than the others. She had to keep an eye on him to make sure he didn't accidentally hurt himself, or do something dangerous, or get lost.

"I think you've got some funny ideas about kids," she said as they drove along. "They're not all little hoodlums, you know."

"No, but a lot of them are, and their mothers are worse," he said matter-of-factly, and she laughed.

"Should I get out of the car now before you find out the truth about me, or will you trust me through dinner?"

"You know what I mean," he insisted. "How many marriages do you know that work, really work?" he asked bluntly, sounding like a true cynic, and a confirmed bachelor.

"My marriage worked," she said simply. "We were very happy for a very long time."

"Well, most people aren't, and you know it," he said, trying to convince her.

"No, you're right, most people aren't that happy, but some are."

"Damn few," he said, as they reached the restaurant, and she looked at him cautiously once they were seated at their table.

"How did you get such terrible views about marriage, Bill? Was it as bad as all that?"

"Worse. By the time it was over, we hated each other. I haven't seen her since, and wouldn't want to. And she'd probably hang up on me, if I called her. That's how bad it was. And I don't think we were the exception." It was obvious that he believed what he was saying, although Liz didn't.

"I think you were," she said calmly.

"If we were, then you'd be out of business." She laughed at that, and they ordered a mushroom-and-pepperoni pizza with olives on it. It sounded good to both of them, and when it came, it was delicious. They dove into it, and had eaten roughly half when they decided they'd had enough, and the waitress served them coffee.

They had talked about a lot of things, medicine, the law, the years he had spent in New York during his residency, and how much he liked it, and she talked about going to Europe with Jack and loving it, particularly Venice. They touched on a wide variety of subjects, but she was still intrigued by what he'd said about marriage and children. He obviously had very strong opinions on the subject. And she felt sorry for him. He had deprived himself of a way of life she cherished. She wouldn't have given up the years of her marriage for anything, and certainly not her children.

Without them, she knew her life would be empty, as she suspected his was. All he really cared about was his work, and the people he took care of and worked with. It was a lot, but not enough for a whole life, in her opinion. But they didn't bring up the subject again. Instead, their conversation turned to films.

He had very eclectic tastes, he liked foreign films, and arty movies, as well as some big commercial ones. She admitted that she enjoyed the kind of movies she saw with her children, they were all very commercial films, and in Peter's case, action movies. And she used to love going with them. It reminded her of how little she had done with her children, out in the world, since Jack died. She was always there for them at home, but she seldom went out with them anymore, and she promised herself silently that she would in future. Bill had gotten her rolling again, and after the film they saw that night, she promised herself she was going to take the kids soon. It was a long time since they had done something like that together, and it was time now.

She invited him in for a drink when they got home, but he said he had to get up early the next day. He had to be at the hospital at six, and she was touched that he had stayed out so late with her. It was after eleven o'clock, and more likely than not, he'd be tired in the morning. She apologized to him for it and he smiled.

"I think you're worth it." She was surprised by his words, but she was glad he said them. She had had a good time with him. She thanked him, he promised to call her again soon, and she went inside as he drove away. Peter and Megan were still up, and she could see almost before she closed the door that she was about to be subjected to the inquisition.

"Did he kiss you?" Megan asked accusingly, with a tone of disapproval and revulsion.

"Of course not. I scarcely know him."

"That wouldn't be cool on the first date," Peter said wisely, and his mother laughed.

"I'm sorry to disappoint you guys, we're just friends. I think he's very careful not to get involved. He cares more about his work. And I care more about you. You have nothing to worry about, Megan," she said firmly.

"I'll bet you ten bucks he kisses you next time," Peter said with a look of amusement.

"You won't win that one," she told him. "Besides, who tells you there'll be a next time? Maybe he had a lousy time and won't call me."

"I doubt it," Megan said glumly. She could see disaster ready to strike them, in the form of Bill Webster.

"Thank you for the vote of confidence, Meg. I wouldn't waste time worrying about it. Besides, I have a trial next week that I'll have to work on."

"Good. You can stay home with us. You don't need a man, Mom."

"Not as long as I have you, is that it, Megan?" But she had to admit, it had been nice being out with Bill, talking about grown-up things and learning about him. There had been just enough of an undercurrent of mutual admiration. They didn't want anything from each other, they just liked each other, and they'd had a good time. Even if she never heard from him again, Liz told herself, it was nice being with him, and feeling like a woman, and not just a mother. It was nice being with someone who wanted her to have a good time, and was interested in talking and listening to her.

She sent Megan and Peter off to bed then, and went to bed herself. Jamie was already in her bed, waiting for her. He still slept with her sometimes, and it was nice being in bed with him too. And as she fell asleep beside her child, she wondered if Megan was right, and she didn't need a man. But she wasn't quite as convinced as she had been. It had been nearly nine months since she lay beside Jack, and had made love with him. It seemed like an eternity to her now, and for the moment at least, she had no real desire to change that. In her mind, that part of her life was over forever.

And as he went to sleep that night, Bill Webster was thinking of her, and how much fun she had been. He wasn't sure what would come of it, but there was no doubt in his mind, he liked her.

Chapter 9

Bill called her again later that week, and invited her to the theater this time. They drove to the city, and had dinner there, and afterwards he came in for a glass of wine, and they talked for a while, about the theater, and books, and she told him about a difficult case she was working on, involving a custody suit and a child she suspected was being abused. She had reported the parents to child protective services, and they had discovered she was right. In some ways, it presented a moral dilemma for her, and she wished that she could represent the child and not the parents.

"Why can't you?" he asked matter-of-factly. It seemed so simple to him, but for her it wasn't.

"It's a little more complicated than that. I'd have to be appointed by the court to represent the child, and I wasn't. I'm considered tainted because I represent the father. And they're right. It would be a conflict of interest for me to represent the child, although I'd much prefer it to representing her father."

"I had a case like that, a kid in the trauma unit who they claimed had been beaten up by a neighbor. They wanted to bring charges against him and they told a very convincing story. I was suitably outraged. Turns out the father was beating the child, and he had brain-damaged her by the time she got to me. There wasn't a hell of a lot we could do about it. They took the child away from them, once she got out of the hospital, but she begged the judge to go back to them. I was afraid the father would kill her. The judge sent her to foster care for a few months, but eventually the child went back to her parents."

"And then what happened?" He had piqued her interest.

"I don't know. I lost track of them, which seemed too bad. My work is so immediate and so acute, once people get well, I lose them. It's the nature of the beast in trauma and emergency. You do what you can in the immediacy of the moment, and then they fade out of your lives."

"Don't you miss having a long-term relationship with your patients?"

"Not really. I think that's part of what I like about it. I don't have to worry about solving problems that aren't really mine to solve, or can't be. This way it's much simpler." He was clearly someone who didn't want long-term relationships of any kind. But she liked him in spite of it. And every now and then, when he said things like that, she felt sorry for him. His life, and philosophies, were everything hers weren't. Everything about her life was long-term and deeply involved. There were clients who stayed in touch with her for years after their divorces. It was just a difference in style, and clearly, she and Bill Webster were very different. But it was equally clear that they liked each other.

It was late again when he left that night. He sat and talked to her till nearly one o'clock, and he was sorry when he left that he couldn't stay longer to talk to her. But they both had to get up early the next day. She had to go to court, and he was due on duty at the trauma unit at seven in the morning.

And Peter had a sly look in his eye when he asked her at breakfast the next day if he'd won his bet.

"No, you lost this time," she smiled, and laughed.

"You mean he didn't kiss you, Mom?" Peter looked disappointed and Megan made a face of utter outrage.

"You're disgusting," she accused him. "Whose side are you on?"

"Mom's," he said clearly, and then he turned back to his mother. "Would you tell the truth if he did, or would you lie just to win the ten bucks?" He loved teasing her, and she laughed as she made them all pancakes.

"Peter, how insulting! I have more integrity than to lie to my own flesh and blood to win a bet." She handed him a plate of pancakes and poured syrup on it.

"I think you're lying, Mom," Peter accused her.

"I'm not. I told you, we're just friends, and I like it like that."

"Keep it that way, Mom," Rachel added. Another country heard from. Liz looked at her youngest daughter with interest.

"When did you get interested in this?"

"Peter says he likes you, and Meg says you're going to marry him." In some ways, she was sophisticated for eleven. She was nearly twelve, but not quite. She had just turned eleven when her father died, and like all of them, she had grown up a lot in the past year, as had their mother.

"Let me reassure you all," she said with a

broad smile, as they finished their breakfast, "two dinners do not constitute an engagement."

"It's too soon for you to be going out," Annie added, looking at her sternly.

"And when do you think it would be appropriate?" her mother asked her with interest.

"Never," Megan answered for her younger sister.

"You're all nuts," Peter said, as he got up from the breakfast table. "Mom can do whatever she wants. And Dad would think it's fine. Dad would be dating by now, if it had happened to Mom instead," and she realized as she listened that by the grace of God it could have. And she thought Peter's comment interesting, as she mulled it over on her way to work. Would Jack have been dating by then if she had died instead? She had never thought about it, but she suspected he might. He had a healthy attitude about life, and too much *joie de vivre* to get buried in a closet, mourning her. Peter was right. Jack probably would have been dating. It made her feel better about seeing Bill Webster.

He called her in the office that day, and asked her to go to the movies with him again the following weekend. They seemed to be seeing a lot of each other suddenly, and she didn't mind. She enjoyed him.

And this time when he came to take her out,

Jamie let him in, and brought him up-to-date on the situation.

"My sisters don't think you should be taking Mom out. But Peter thinks it's all right, and so do I. The boys like you, and the girls don't." He summed it up for him nicely, and Bill laughed out loud and mentioned it to her on the way to a small French restaurant in Sausalito.

"Are they really upset that we're dating?" he asked with interest.

"Are we?" Liz asked easily. "I thought we were just friends."

"Is that what you want, Liz?" he asked her gently. They were at the restaurant by then, and he had just pulled into the parking lot as he turned to look at her. He was anxious to hear how she answered the question.

"I'm not sure what I want," she said honestly. "I have a good time with you. This just kind of happened." It was how he felt as well, but he was beginning to feel more for her than he'd expected. At first, he would have been satisfied to be her friend, but now he wasn't as sure. He was beginning to think he wanted more from her. But they didn't press the point any further, as they walked into the restaurant, and stayed off heavy subjects for the rest of the evening.

But this time, when he took her home, Peter would have won the bet, if there had still been one. Just before Bill walked her into the house, he pulled her carefully into his arms, and with a look of tenderness in his eyes, he kissed her. She looked a little startled at first, and then she relaxed in his arms, and kissed him back, but afterwards she looked sad, and he was worried.

"Are you all right, Liz?" he whispered.

"I think so," she said softly. For a flash of an instant, kissing him made her think of Jack, and she almost felt as though she were cheating on him. She wasn't hungry for a man, she hadn't been looking for anyone, but Bill Webster had walked into her life, and now she had to deal with her feelings about him, and her late husband. "I didn't expect that," she said, turning to look at him, and he nodded.

"Neither did I. It just kind of happened. You're an amazing woman."

"No, I'm not," she smiled at him, as they lingered outside. It was nice to be out in the fresh air, and not within earshot of her children. It would have made her uncomfortable if they had been aware of what had just happened. And as though to reinforce what they had both felt that night, he kissed her again, and this time she kissed him back with greater fervor. She was breathless when they stopped and a little worried. "What are we doing?" she asked, as they stood beneath the stars of a September night, and he smiled at her.

"I think we're kissing," he said simply. But it was much more than that, it wasn't just idle curiosity, or the hunger of two lonely bodies, it was the clear attraction that happened sometimes between a man and a woman, a meeting of minds as well as lips. There were a great many things they liked about each other, although they had already agreed that they were very different. He liked fleeting relationships of all kinds, and everything in her life was based on permanence, marriage, children, career, even her two employees had worked for her for years. There was nothing temporary in her life, and he knew that about her. It was almost a challenge to him to be different. But he wasn't sure now if he wanted to be temporary in her life either. This was a new experience for him, but she wasn't the kind of woman he usually was attracted to. "Let's take this slow," he said to her, "and not think about it too much. Let's just see what happens." She nodded, not sure what to say to him, or if anything more should happen.

But by the time she was in the house again, and he was gone, she was consumed by guilt over what she'd done. She felt as though she had betrayed her husband. But he's gone, she told herself, and he was never coming back. But then why did it feel so strange to be kissing Bill, and so wrong, and at the same time so exciting? It unnerved her as she thought about it, and she lay awake for a long time that night, thinking about him, and Jack, and wondering what she was doing.

And the next morning, when she woke up, tired from a long, sleepless night, she told herself that they would have to go back to their easy friendship, without adding complications to it. She felt better when she decided that, until he called her at ten o'clock that morning.

"I was thinking about you, and I thought I'd call and see how you were," he said gently.

"I'm sorry about last night," she said simply.

"What were you sorry about?" he asked, sounding strangely calm and more than a little happy. "I was only sorry that we didn't kiss again. That was pretty great stuff, as far as I'm concerned."

"That's what I was afraid of. Bill . . . I'm not ready. . . ."

"I understand. No one's pushing. This is not a race. We don't have to 'get' anywhere. We're just there for each other." It was a nice way to put it, and she was grateful that he didn't press her. It made her feel a little silly for being so worried.

"How about if I come and cook dinner for you and the kids on Saturday? I have a night off, and I'm a pretty fair cook. How about it?" She knew that she should turn him down, but was surprised to find she didn't want to. And what harm could there be in letting him cook for them?

"All right. I'll help you."

"I'll bring the groceries. Is there anything special the children like?"

"They eat anything, chicken, fish, steak, pizza, spaghetti. They're easy."

"I'll think of something."

"Jamie will be thrilled." And the girls would hate it, but she didn't say that. It was a good opportunity to encourage them to relax about him. They could see how harmless he was, or was he? Were they right after all that this was a potentially dangerous situation? She hated to think that. She wanted to be his friend, and she liked kissing him. But did it have to be more than that? She couldn't see why. Maybe they could just keep it to kissing. She certainly wasn't going to let it go further than that, for her own sake, not her children's.

He arrived at six o'clock on Saturday night, as promised, with three bags of groceries. He said he was going to cook them southern fried chicken, corn on the cob, and baked potatoes.

He had brought some ice cream bars too. And as he buzzed around her kitchen, he wouldn't let her help him.

"You relax," he told her. He handed her a glass of wine, poured one for himself, and proceeded to cook them an excellent dinner. Even the girls were surprised and pleased when they ate it, although Megan continued to refuse to speak to him. But Jamie chatted with him throughout the meal, and Peter did too, and eventually Annie and Rachel joined the conversation. They were talking about schools, and colleges for Peter. He had set a date for his college tour with Liz, in early October, and Bill gave him what advice he could. Although he thought Berkeley might be fun, he felt Stanford and UCLA the better choices for him, for a variety of reasons. And they were still discussing it at the end of the meal when Rachel, Annie, Jamie, and Liz cleared the table. Peter was still deeply engrossed in conversation with Bill, and Megan slipped upstairs without thanking him for dinner, and Liz was furious with her. But afterwards, Bill told Liz not to push her.

"She'll get used to me, give her time. There's no rush." He kept saying things like that, and they always made Liz faintly nervous. Why did they have to give her time? Surely he was not going to stick around long enough for it to matter. But that was not what he had been hinting.

He kissed her again that night, after all the kids went to bed, and it made her nervous to kiss him in her house. This was getting very cozy, and a little too familiar. And he had been very nice to her children. It had all the makings of a full-scale romance. Jack had been gone for nine months by then, and she was beginning to feel as though she were walking through a mine field, which might explode at any moment. Megan was poised for attack, the other girls were unsure, and more than anything, Liz had her own emotions to deal with, her concerns about Bill, and his propensity for temporary attachments, by his own admission, and her sense of loyalty to Jack, which was being severely challenged by her feelings for Bill Webster.

She felt that way all through September and into October, and it was a relief when she left for the weekend on the college tour with Peter. But in spite of that, Bill was calling every day, and even called her at the hotel in Los Angeles where they were staying. It was a surprise to hear from him, but she was smiling when she hung up, and this time Peter didn't comment. He didn't want to say anything to upset the delicate balance of their romance, mostly because he liked him, and wanted it to work out between them. And he knew from little things she said how ambivalent his mother was feeling.

When they got back, she waited a few days before she saw Bill, and then only for a quick hamburger in the cafeteria on a night he was on duty at the hospital, but Bill had been anxious to see her. The nurses all recognized her, and some came over to say hello, as did the chief resident, and everyone said to say hello to Peter.

"Everybody loves you, Liz." She had made a big impression on everyone with her devotion to Peter. Not all parents were as attentive as she was, in fact few were. And she was attentive to Bill too, always asking him questions about his work, and concerned about him, and the challenges and stresses he faced daily. When he was with her, he was always aware of how much she cared about him, sometimes more than she was. She had a hard time admitting that to herself. It still had too many implications.

It wasn't a coincidence when, the following week, early on a Saturday morning, after they came back from L.A., she stood quietly on Jack's side of their closet, looking at the jackets that still hung there. They looked lifeless now, and sad, and it depressed her to see them. She didn't hold them close to her anymore, or stroke them as she once had, or try to imagine him as she clung to them. It had been several months since she held his lapels to her face and smelled them, and as she looked at them now, she knew what she had to do, for her own sake. It had nothing to do with Bill, she told herself. It had been ten months since Jack died, and she was ready. And one by one she took the jackets off the hangers, and folded them in a neat pile. She would have offered them to Peter, but he was too tall and too young to wear them, and it was easier to dispose of them than to see someone else wear them.

It had taken her two hours to empty the drawers and the hanging part of the closet, when Megan walked into her room and saw what she was doing. Megan started to cry, and for an instant Liz felt as though she had killed him. Megan stood there staring at the neat piles of his clothes on the floor and sobbed, and as Liz looked at her she started crying, for her children, for him, for herself. But no matter what she hung on to now, they had lost him. He wasn't coming back, and he didn't need the clothes anymore. It was better to give his things away, she told herself, but as she saw Megan's distress over it, she wondered.

"Why are you doing that now? It's because of *him*, isn't it?" They both knew she meant Bill, and Liz shook her head, as they both stood in the walk-in closet crying.

Danielle Steel

"It's time, Meg. . . . I had to. . . . It hurts
me too much to see them," Liz said, as she cried
and reached out to her daughter, but Megan
pulled away, ran to her room, and slammed the
door, and a few minutes later, Liz followed. But
Megan didn't want to talk to her, and Liz went
back to her own room, to put Jack's clothes in
boxes. Peter walked by her room and saw what
she was doing, stopped and looked at her, and
then quietly offered to help her.

"I'll do it for you, Mom. You don't have to do
that."

"I want to," she said sadly. It was the last rem-
nant of him that he had left behind, other than
his trophies, and his photographs, and a few me-
mentos, and of course their children.

Peter helped her take it all out to the car, and
as though sensing that a turning point had come,
one by one the children came and watched her.
There was a look of loss evident in their eyes, and
at the very last, Megan came out of her room and
looked at her mother. It was obvious that it wasn't
easy for Liz either, and then, as a silent move of
support for her, each of the children picked
something up, a box, a bag, a coat, and carried it
to the car. It was a last gesture of good-bye to
their father. And at the very end, Megan came,
carrying the last armload.

"I'm sorry, Mom," she whispered through

her tears, and Liz turned and clung to her, grateful for the bond between them.

"I love you, Meg." Mother and daughter cried as they held each other, and the others were crying too by the time the car was full.

"I love you too, Mom," Megan said softly, and the others came to hug her.

She was taking the clothes to a local charity drop, and Peter offered to drive her.

"I'm okay. I can do it alone," she reassured him. He was wearing a smaller neck brace by then, and had just begun to drive again, and he insisted on driving her. She was too upset to drive the car and she knew it. And together, they drove slowly out of the driveway, with the car piled high with his father's things, as the others watched.

They were back half an hour later, and Liz looked ravaged, and when she walked back into her closet that afternoon and saw the empty space, her heart gave a little tug, remembering what had been there, but she felt freer. It had taken her a long time, but she knew she had been right to wait until she was ready, despite the endless advice she'd been given about when to put away Jack's clothes.

She sat in her room for a long time, staring out the window, and thinking of him, and when Bill called late that afternoon, he could hear in her voice that something had happened.

"Are you okay?" He sounded worried.

"More or less." She told him what she had done that day, and how hard it had been, and his heart ached as he listened. In the past two months, he had come to care about her deeply.

"I'm sorry, Liz." He knew it was a sign of some kind, a symbol of the fact that she was slowly letting go of the past, and saying a last good-bye to her husband. He would always be a part of her, and their children were his legacy, but she was loosing her grip on his reality and daily presence. "Can I do anything?"

"No," she said sadly, they both knew it was a private agony, and a solitary moment.

"I was going to ask you if you wanted to go out tonight, but maybe that's not such a great idea." She agreed with him, and he said he'd call her in the morning. In the end, he called her again later that night, just to see how she was. She still sounded sad, but a little better, and she'd spent a quiet evening with the children. They had all calmed down after the sorrow of the morning. And only Liz was left with her memories, and her sense of loss. The others seemed to have come to terms with it long before she had.

The next day when he called, she sounded more herself again, and he was pleased when she agreed to see him that evening. She seemed quieter than usual, and more subdued, but after they talked for a while, she was laughing again, and seemed in better spirits.

They went for a long, quiet walk, and held hands, and when he kissed her this time, they both knew it was different. She was ready to face the future, to let go of the past, and move forward.

"I love you, Liz," he said, as he held her close to him, and she smelled his now-familiar aftershave. He was so different from Jack in so many ways, and she cared for him, but she could not bring herself to say the words. Not yet. And maybe never.

"I know," was all she said, and he didn't expect more of her. It was enough for both of them for now that he had said it.

Chapter 10

By Halloween, they both knew it was serious.
Neither of them had come to terms with it, or
figured out what it meant for their future, but Bill
was obviously in love with her, and although she
didn't admit it to him yet, she knew that she loved
him. It was a dilemma for her, because she didn't
know what to do about it, or what to tell her children. She had talked to Victoria about it more
than once, and her only advice had been to go
slow and let things "unfold," which sounded sensible to Liz, and it was what she thought too. She
knew that in time, they'd both know how they
felt, and what to do.

Bill came to the house and they took Rachel
and Jamie trick-or-treating. Annie and Megan

said they were "too old" to go trick-or-treating, and stayed home to hand out candy at the door with Carole. Peter was at his new girlfriend's house, handing out trick-or-treat candy there.

And late that night, when the children were in bed, Bill looked at her quietly, and asked her if she would go away with him for the weekend. She hesitated for a long time, and he was suddenly terrified that he had ruined everything, but they had been dating for two months, and their passion had become harder and harder to restrain. He knew that he hadn't misinterpreted what she felt for him, and his own feelings were clear, at least to him. And he felt like a kid again when she quietly said she'd go to the Napa Valley with him the following weekend. They agreed not to tell the kids, and he said he'd make reservations for them. He wanted to take her to the Auberge du Soleil, because it was the most romantic place he could think of for their first weekend together.

Bill picked her up late Friday afternoon, he had been working since the night before, but he was so happy and excited that he wasn't tired. And Liz had made lots of plans for the children that weekend to keep them busy. She had told them she was going to stay with a friend from law school, and she had arranged a time with Bill to pick her up when she knew everyone would be out. Only Carole knew where she was really going. And Bill was faintly amused by her modesty and discretion, but he also knew that it was easier for them both that way. There was no need to upset her kids. Although Peter and Jamie might have been pleased to know they were going away together, the girls most certainly wouldn't. There was still plenty of resistance among them being generated by Megan. She was civil to him by then, but barely more than that, and there was no reason to antagonize her further.

The scenery was beautiful along the way, the leaves had turned a variety of coppery colors, and the grass was still green, as it always was in winter. It was an odd combination of East and West, the fall colors of New England, combined with the evergreen of California. And they chatted all the way to Saint Helena. Liz was quiet from time to time, and he didn't want to ask her what she was thinking. He knew that being with him was still an adjustment for her, and she had told him more than once that there were times when she felt as though she were betraying Jack. He knew that in some ways, this weekend wouldn't be easy for her. And as they drove along, Liz glanced at the wedding ring she was still wearing.

They checked into the room close to dinnertime, and Liz was touched when she saw how elegant it was. He had gone all out to spoil her and make her happy. And the view of the valley stretching endlessly before her at dusk took her breath away. She went into the bathroom to change after Bill poured them both some wine, and came out in a new black dress for dinner.

They ate in the hotel's dining room, and afterwards went to sit in front of the fireplace at the bar, while a woman sang at the piano. And they were both comfortable and relaxed as they wandered slowly back to their room. They held hands, and as soon as they walked in, Bill kissed her. It was a kiss that told her everything she meant to him, and within minutes, they were both swept away by their passion for each other. There was a fire burning in the fireplace, the lights were low, and Bill lit the candles on the coffee table, and then they sat down on the couch with their arms around each other. And slowly, he peeled the black dress away, as she unbuttoned his shirt. It was wonderful to be there alone, and have the freedom to do whatever they wanted. And then gently, he led her toward the bed. He undressed her slowly and sensually, and they slipped into the clean sheets naked and lay there for a long minute, just holding each other.

"I love you so much, Liz. . . ."

"I love you too . . ." she whispered to him. It was the first time she had actually said the words to him, but this time they came easily to her, as easily as what came next, as they kissed and then finally gave in to their passion. She was swept away by him and the longing she had felt for him, and suddenly all the sorrow and loneliness and fear seemed to fall away, like a cocoon she had wrapped herself in and no longer needed to protect her. She needed no protection from him, there was no place to hide, nothing she held back from him, as she gave herself to him. And afterwards, they lay breathless and sated and she smiled at him, but there was something bittersweet and nostalgic in her eyes, and he knew that the past and the memories still had their fingertips on her heart. It would have been impossible for it to be any different, and they both knew that.

"Are you okay?" he asked gently, worried about her, and sorry that she still looked so sad. But no matter what he saw in her eyes, she was smiling at him.

"I'm fine . . . better than that . . . you make me so happy."

It was almost true, as true as it could be at the moment.

He saw that there were tears in her eyes. It was hard not to think of Jack at moments like this, as she gave herself to someone else. It was another important step away from him, a step she had postponed for as long as possible, but that she wanted to take now. It was like walking across a bridge from one life to the next. But she felt safe with Bill, and she could tell him anything. He wasn't wounded or upset because she admitted that it wasn't easy for her.

They lay side by side in bed for a long time, talking about things, and he admitted that he had never loved anyone as he loved her. And she lay peacefully beside him, enjoying being with him, and trying to force herself not to think of Jack. But it was hard not to think of him, and Bill was sensitive to her feelings.

As the weekend unfolded, she was less and less aware of Jack, and more and more aware of Bill and all that she shared with him. They went for long walks, and talked about a variety of things, their work, her children, their dreams. They avoided talking about the past as much as possible, and inevitably on Sunday morning, as they sat on the deck of their room, looking out over the Napa Valley, their conversation drifted slowly toward the future.

He was wearing a sweatshirt and jeans, and she was wearing a cozy wool bathrobe in the cool November morning. The day was warm, and it was pleasant just sitting there, basking in the sun, as they shared the paper. And when Liz glanced up at him and handed him the sports section, he was smiling at her.

"What are you looking so happy about, Dr.

Webster?" She smiled at him as he took the paper from her.

"You. This." He gestured toward the valley. The whole weekend had had the feeling of a honeymoon to both of them, and in some of the more important ways, she was his now. Jack was drifting slowly into the mists behind her. And although part of her still wanted to hold on to him, and always would, she knew she had to move on. And Bill was a wonderful companion to her. "What are we going to do about us?" he asked her gently.

"What does that mean?" She looked suddenly worried as he said it. They were words she was not yet ready to hear, and he knew that, but he couldn't help it. It had been on his mind since they started dating. "We don't have to do anything," she said, sounding nervous.

"It might be nice though. Is it too soon to talk about that, Liz?" They had made love again the day before, and at night in front of the fire, and again that morning. They were amazingly compatible, and it was hard to believe they had never made love before that weekend. Everything about them seemed to mesh and blend, and be just what they both needed and wanted. It was hard to ignore that. "I never thought I'd be saying this to you," he went on, suddenly feeling

young and awkward, but he was so in love with
her he didn't want to lose her. "But I think eventually we ought to get married." She was shocked
when he actually said it. She had never expected
him to say that, it was completely out of character
for him.

"I thought you didn't believe in marriage."
She looked as though she wanted a recount, and
he could see that she was frightened by what he
had said.

"I didn't, until I met you. I guess this is why,
because somewhere in my heart, I hoped it could
be like this one day, and I didn't want to waste my
tickets with someone it wouldn't work with, like
my first wife. We damn near annihilated each
other." But in his eyes at least, this was perfect.
And she could see being with him for a long time,
maybe forever, but she was not yet ready to say it.
It was too soon for her, and the memories of Jack
were still too fresh. It hadn't been a year yet, although it was close to it. "I don't want to blow
anything by talking about this too soon, Liz, but I
wanted you to know that this is the direction I'm
headed." She wasn't a woman one took lightly,
and there were her kids to think of. He had
thought about them a lot, and knew he could
come to love them. He already did love Jamie,
and had a strong bond with Peter. And he figured

the girls would come around eventually. He had never had a problem winning over women and children, when he cared to, and in this case he did.

"I don't know what to say." She had friends who went out with men for years who never took them seriously, never proposed, and had no desire to, and she had just spent her first weekend with him, and he was talking about the future. "It's only been eleven months since Jack died. That's not very long. I need time to readjust and get back on my feet again, and so do the kids."

"I know. I'm not in a hurry. And I know how important the year is to you." She talked about it a lot, and it was a milestone she obviously respected, as did her children. And he had to respect it with her. "I was hoping we could talk about it again in January, after the holidays, and see how you were feeling. I was kind of hoping that Valentine's Day . . ." Her heart gave a little tug as his voice drifted off. Valentine's Day had meant a great deal to her and Jack. But so many things had, and they were gone now, except for the children.

"That's just three months away," she said with a look of panic. But it meant a lot to her too that he was asking.

"We'll have known each other for six months

by then. It's fast, but respectable. A lot of people know each other for less, and have very happy marriages." She knew that was true, but she and Jack had known each other for a long time. And she had been unprepared for what Bill was saying to her. She wasn't averse to it, but she needed time to think it over. He looked at her then, with everything he felt for her in his eyes. "I'll do whatever you want, Liz. I just want you to know how much I love you."

"I love you too, and I feel very lucky. Some people aren't that lucky once, I've been blessed twice, but I still need some time to get over what happened."

"I know that. I'm not rushing you. But I guess what I want to know is if, in time, you might want the same future I do."

"I think so," she smiled shyly, and then took a breath and let her emotions rule her for a moment. "I just need time to get there. Let's talk about it again after Christmas." She wanted to honor the year, for Jack's sake, and her own, and the children's.

"That's all I wanted to know," he said gently, and took her hand from across the table. "I love you. I'm not going anywhere. We've got all the time in the world to put this together. As long as it's what we both want, there's no hurry." He was reasonable and kind and compassionate, she couldn't have wanted more from any man, and she wasn't even sure Jack would have been as understanding. He was far more impatient and stubborn, and less willing to follow her lead. More often than not, it was Jack who determined both their pace and their direction. In some ways, it was more of a partnership with Bill, and she liked that.

They drove slowly back to Tiburon that afternoon, and the children were all home when they arrived. She could see Megan raise an eyebrow when she got out of Bill's car, but nothing was said until later that evening, when the younger children were in bed and Peter was busy doing his homework in his room.

"Why were you in Bill's car?" Megan finally confronted her in her bedroom that night. "Did you spend the weekend with him?" Liz hesitated for a moment, and then nodded. If she was going to marry him eventually, which was the direction they seemed to be heading in, from everything they'd said over the weekend, she wanted to be honest with her daughter.

"Yes, I did. We went to the Napa Valley."

"Mom!" Megan shouted at her. "That's *disgusting*!"

"Why? He cares about me a great deal, and I

care about him, there's nothing wrong with that, Meg. We're not hurting anyone. I think we love each other." But it was a heavy dose for her daughter to swallow.

"What about Daddy?" There were tears in her eyes when she said it.

"Daddy's gone, Meg. I loved him with all my heart and always will. This isn't the same, it's different, for me, and for all of us. But I'm not going to be alone for the rest of my life. I have a right to someone in my life." She spoke to her daughter as gently as she could, but it needed to be said.

"That's *sick!*" Megan chastised her, furious with her mother. "It hasn't even been a year since Daddy died. I never knew you were a slut before, Mom." Her eyes were blazing and Liz stood up in anger as she said it. She had never laid a hand on her and she didn't intend to start now, but she wasn't going to let her behave that way either.

"Don't speak to me that way. Now go to your room until you can be civil. If you want to talk about it with me, you can, but you can't be disrespectful."

"I have no reason to respect you!" Megan said grandly from the safety of the doorway, and then slammed the door, and ran into Peter's room and told him what had happened. But instead of sympathizing with her, he called her a bitch and told her to apologize to her mother. "Whose side are you on anyway?"

"Hers," he said bluntly, "she's done everything for us, and she loved Dad just as much as we did. But she's all alone, there's no one to help her or take care of her, she works like a dog for us, and to keep Dad's law office open. And besides, Bill's a nice guy and I like him. We could do a lot worse, so if you want to know whose side I'm on, I'm on their side. Don't ask me for sympathy if you're acting like shit with Mom, Meg."

"You're an asshole!" she shouted at him, with tears brimming in her eyes. "And besides, she has us, she doesn't need some guy to sleep with."

"She can't sleep with Jamie for the rest of her life. What happens when we go to college? I'll be gone next year, you'll be gone in two years. Then what? She's supposed to sit here waiting for us to come home from school so she has a life again? She has no life without Dad, Meg. Look at her, all she does is work and drive carpool. She deserves better than that, and you know it."

"Not yet," Megan said, overwhelmed by what he'd said, as she sat down on his bed and started crying. "It's too soon. I'm not ready." He sat down next to her and put his arms around her then, he had grown up immeasurably in the past year, even more so since his accident, and they all knew it. "I miss Daddy," she wailed, sounding like Jamie.

"So do I," Peter said, fighting back tears of his own. No matter how much he had grown up, or how sensible he was, he still missed him. "But whether or not Bill is here, it won't change that. Nothing will. We just have to accept what happened."

"I don't want to," she wailed, getting mascara all over his T-shirt. "I want him back." There was nothing he could say to her, he just held her while she cried, and they both thought about their father.

And finally, after Peter talked to her for a while when she had calmed down, Megan went and apologized to her mother. She stood awkwardly in the doorway, after opening it without knocking.

"I don't like him, but I'm sorry for what I said about you." It was the best she could offer, and her mother acknowledged the apology with a serious expression.

"I'm sorry you're so unhappy, Meg. I know this isn't easy."

"You don't know what it's like for us, you have him now," she said accusingly, and Liz sighed as she looked at her.

"Being with Bill doesn't make me miss Daddy any less. Sometimes it makes me miss him more.

This isn't easy for any of us. And I know how hard it is for all of you." It was getting better for all of them, but slowly.

"Do you really love him, Mom?" Megan still looked horrified by what her mother had said, and she wished she'd never heard the words.

"I think I do," Liz said honestly. "I need time to figure it out. He's a nice man. That's all I know right now. I still have a lot to sort out about Daddy."

"It seems like you want to forget him," Megan said sadly.

"I can never forget him, Meg. No matter what I do, or where I go. . . . I loved him for half my life, and we had all of you . . . things just happened. It wasn't fair, for any of us. But now we have to make the best of it, and go on, the way he would want us to."

"You're just saying that to make yourself feel better."

"No, I'm saying it because I believe it."

Megan just shook her head then, and went back to her own room. Her mother had given her a lot to think about, and she didn't even want to share it with her sisters. And after Megan left the room, Liz went quietly to the jewel box she kept in her closet, and took off the wedding ring Jack had once placed on her finger, and she felt as though she were ripping her heart out as she did it. But she knew that the time had come. Peter noticed it the next morning, but said nothing to his mother or the others, although it even made him sad to see it.

But for the next two weeks, whenever Bill came to pick Liz up, Megan was a little more respectful. She didn't say much to him, but she wasn't rude to him either, and Liz was grateful. It was the best she could hope for, for the moment. Jamie and Peter were still his most ardent fans among the kids.

Liz was spending a lot of time with Bill, and they went to his apartment and made love whenever he had some time and was off duty. Sometimes they spent time together when he was on call, and he would have to leap out of bed and grab the phone, but Liz never objected. She had a strong respect for his work, more than for her own these days. She had told him more than once that her family law practice depressed her. She no longer seemed to enjoy what she was doing. It had been fun with Jack, but it wasn't anymore. It seemed frivolous and argumentative and so pointless. The only thing she really liked these days was structuring good custody arrangements for people's children.

"Maybe I'm losing it," she said to him one day when they met in the hospital cafeteria for a sandwich. She had just been to court, and she was furious with one of her clients, who had behaved like a boor to his wife in court in front of the judge. She had been tempted to walk off the case, but she hadn't. "I don't even enjoy going to court anymore."

"Maybe you just need a breather." She'd only had two weeks off in the past year, she worked weekends and nights, and she was carrying a double workload.

"Maybe I should go to beauty school and get a job in a beauty parlor. It might be more useful."

"Don't be so hard on yourself," he smiled at her, but she still looked unhappy.

"Jack loved family law work, it was really more his thing than mine. I just got good at it from working with him. But I don't know now. . . ." She was one of the best divorce lawyers in the area, and it was hard to believe she didn't like it. Her clients would have been stunned by what she was saying. She was always so full of energy, bright ideas and creative suggestions. But lately, she felt like a windup doll whose batteries had run down. She didn't enjoy it anymore, and she wasn't happy. But she felt she owed it to Jack to keep going, for him.

She asked Bill what he was doing for Thanksgiving. They had talked about it once before, and he wasn't sure if he'd be working. He had just found out that he had the day off, and he wouldn't even be on call. He was free to do whatever he wanted, but he hadn't made any plans since he had expected to be working over the holiday.

"Why don't you spend it with us?" Liz said easily. The children were getting used to him, and it might be a nice way to break everyone in, she thought, over the holidays. They all loved Thanksgiving, or at least they had, when their father was alive. Liz knew it would be different this year, for all of them and her too. And trying to keep the tension level down, she had discouraged her mother from coming out.

But she wasn't prepared for the children's reaction when she told them that Bill would be joining them. Megan had a fit, predictably, Rachel and Annie said that he wasn't part of the family and didn't belong there, and even Jamie looked a little startled. She talked to Peter about asking Bill not to come, but he thought that would be mean, and he thought it might be nice to have him. And in the end, she didn't say anything to Bill about their reaction. She just hoped they'd settle down, and be good sports when the day came, but she realized on Thanksgiving Day that her optimism had been unfounded. When the doorbell rang and he arrived, all three girls were still very angry with her.

Bill walked in wearing a tweed jacket, gray

slacks, and a red tie, and Liz was wearing a brown velvet pantsuit. The children were all neatly dressed, and Peter was wearing the same suit he'd worn at his father's funeral, Jamie his gray flannels and blazer. They were a handsome group, and as Liz poured Bill a glass of wine, she was suddenly glad that he had joined them. She realized suddenly how empty the table would seem to all of them without their father there. It would have turned into another mournful memory of him, and this way they had to keep up a good front, and talk to Bill, and each other.

They sat down to their Thanksgiving meal at five o'clock as they always did, and she said grace, as they bowed their heads. She thanked God for the many blessings they shared, the people at their table, and those who were absent, and specifically Jack. There was a long moment of silence after she said it, and Megan looked pointedly at Bill Webster. And then Liz said "Amen" and went out to the kitchen with Peter to get the turkey.

Peter was seated at the head of the table, which reminded everyone again that things were different, and the new face seated next to Liz emphasized it even further.

The bird itself was a splendid specimen, and Liz had cooked it to perfection. Carole was off for the weekend, and the girls had helped her make the stuffing. Rachel particularly liked to cook, and Jamie had helped them. But when Peter tried to carve, he proved to be hopelessly inept, and Liz had never been good at carving. Bill stepped to the head of the table with a smile.

"Let me give you a hand, son," he said amiably. He was enjoying the family scene around the table. It had been years since he'd celebrated a real Thanksgiving. He was always working. But his choice of words had run through Megan's heart like a sword, and she spoke barely audibly but loud enough for Bill to hear her.

"He's not your son," she said in a venomous tone. Bill looked surprised and glanced at Liz, and then turned to Megan.

"I'm sorry, Megan. I didn't mean to offend anyone." There was total silence then as he carved the bird, and he was good at it. And as Liz handed out their full plates she chatted a little too much and a little too hard to compensate for the awkward moment. But by the time Bill sat down again, everyone had calmed down.

The table was quieter than usual this year. It was their first Thanksgiving without their father, and everyone was aware that the agony of Christmas was coming.

Bill asked if they'd done their Christmas shopping yet, and everyone looked mournful at the question. They were not an easy group to entertain, but eventually Jamie made them laugh at something he said, and Annie chimed in, and reminded them of the year that Dad had dropped the turkey on the kitchen floor while he was carving it, and no one had told Mom. She never knew it had slid halfway across the floor before she served it.

Bill laughed along with them, and Liz poured him another glass of wine, and when they took the plates out to the kitchen and brought back the pies, Rachel said loudly that he drank too much, and Bill heard her.

"It's okay, Rachel, I'm not on call today," he said with a warm smile, but she didn't respond, and he went on talking to Jamie. Bill was certainly not drunk, but he'd had three glasses of wine by then and seemed comfortable and happy. He'd been talking to Jamie about football.

"Dad hated football." Megan added insult to injury, she was goading him, and they all knew it.

"I'm sorry to hear that, Meg. It's a great sport. I used to play in college."

"Dad said only morons and brutes play football," she said then, stepping over the line, and her mother was quick to stop her.

"Megan, that's enough!"

"Yes, it is, Mom!" She threw down her napkin

and stood up with tears in her eyes. "Why does he have to be here with us? He's not our father, he's just your boyfriend."

The other children looked stunned, and Liz was shaking as she answered. "Bill's our friend, and it's Thanksgiving. That's what Thanksgiving is about, friends joined around a table to give thanks, and to join hands in friendship."

"Is that what you do with him? 'Join hands'? I'll bet you do a lot more than that, and I'll bet Daddy hates you for it," she said, and then ran up the stairs to her room and slammed the door, as Peter leaned over and apologized for her. But one by one, Rachel and Annie left the table too, as Jamie helped himself to a slice of apple pie while no one was looking. It looked too good to waste, and no one else could think about eating.

"So much for family holidays," Bill said with a grim look, as Liz looked at him in devastation. She realized now that she had been ambitious in inviting him, and including him in the family wasn't going to be as easy as he had hoped. In fact, she understood all too well now, it was going to be a nightmare.

"I'll go up and talk to her," Peter said, looking embarrassed for all of them, and then to Bill, "I'm sorry about my sisters."

"Don't worry about it. I understand." But in

fact, he didn't. He was looking tense and grim when he glanced at Liz, dabbing at her eyes with her napkin.

"I guess this is harder for them than I thought."

"It wasn't exactly a picnic for me either, Liz," he said bluntly. "The role of intruder isn't one I wear very well, I'm afraid. They act like I'm an ax murderer, or as if I killed their father." His ego was bruised, and his feelings had taken a beating at her children's hands, and he had no one to take it out on but her. Everyone was angry at her. Bill, and three of her children. Only Jamie looked unconcerned as he kept on eating. There was no one else left at the table.

"You have to understand how hard this is for them. It's their first Thanksgiving without their father."

"I know that, Liz. But that's not my fault." He raised his voice to her as he said it, and Jamie looked at him in consternation.

"No one said it was, but you're here and he's not. This is all my fault. I probably shouldn't have asked you," Liz said, still crying, as Jamie watched them in silence.

"And what about next year? I'll make sure to sign up for a seventy-two-hour stretch at the hospital over Thanksgiving. It's obvious I won't be welcome here, at least not till your kids leave home." He was overwhelmed by his own anger.

"Are you coming for Thanksgiving next year?" Jamie asked with interest.

"I was planning to, but now I'm not so sure," he snapped at the child and then hated himself for it. He reached out and touched Jamie's hand, and lowered his voice again so he didn't scare him. "I'm sorry . . . I'm just upset."

"Megan was rude to Mom," Jamie said matter-of-factly. "And so was Annie. Don't they like you?" He looked sad for his friend, and Liz saw Bill's jaw tense when he answered.

"I guess not. I guess that's the crux of it, isn't it?" He directed his question at Liz, who wanted desperately to reassure him. "I guess I'm *persona non grata* here, and I'm kidding myself if I think it's ever going to be any different. As Megan said so succinctly at the beginning of the meal, I'm not their father, and I never will be."

"No one's expecting you to be," Liz said in the calmest voice she could muster. "All you have to be is their friend. No one's expecting you to fill Jack's shoes," she said softly, fighting back her own tears, as he glowered at her.

"Maybe I am, Liz. Maybe that's the problem. Maybe I was deluding myself that I could be important to you, and to them, instead of just an interloper, always playing second best to him. What was it Megan said, 'a brute and a moron'?"

"She was just trying to provoke you." Her loyalty was to her children, but to him too. It was a ghastly situation for her.

"Well, she succeeded very nicely. In fact," he stood up and put his napkin down on the table, "I think I'll give you all some relief, and myself. I think it's time for me to go back to work."

"I thought you weren't working today," she said, looking confused and upset. He had told her he was off for the holiday, which was how it had all started.

"I think I'll go back anyway. At least I know what I'm doing there. I think family scenes, particularly on holidays, aren't my strong suit." In truth, he had done fine, but the deck had been stacked against him, and he knew it. It had been a no-win situation right from the beginning. He looked at Liz from where he stood, and neither of them moved, but she knew that something terrible was happening, and they were both afraid to say it. "Thanks for dinner, Liz. I'll call you." And without another word, he walked out the front door and slammed it behind him, as she sat staring at it.

Jamie looked up at her then, having finished his pie, and commented on the situation. "He forgot to say good-bye to me. Is he mad at me?"

"No, sweetheart. He's mad at me. Your sisters were very rude to him."

"Are you going to spank them?" She smiled at the question. She never had, and she wasn't planning to start now at their age, but the suggestion was certainly tempting.

"No, but someone should."

"Santa Claus is going to put coal in their stockings," Jamie said with a solemn look, and Liz smiled sadly. Just thinking about Christmas made her shudder. It was the anniversary of Jack's death, and she realized that under no circumstances could she include Bill in what they were doing. The Thanksgiving they had just experienced had taught her a painful lesson.

She and Jamie cleared the rest of the table then, and afterwards she went upstairs to talk to her daughters. Peter was sitting with all of them, and it was obvious that Megan had been crying.

"I hate him!" She spat at her mother, but Liz managed to stay calm in spite of the havoc she had caused. She knew what was behind it.

"I don't think you do, Meg. What's to hate? He's a nice man, even if he did play football in college. What you hate is the fact that your father's gone. So do I. But there's nothing we can do about it. And it's not Bill's fault. I shouldn't have invited him to join us today, and I'm sorry."

Peter touched her arm with a gentle smile.

He admired her so much, she was always straight with them, and he knew how much she loved them. She had been there for him in every possible way after his accident that summer. And he was sorry for her that their Thanksgiving had been such a disaster, and that Bill had been Megan's scapegoat. Like Liz, he understood perfectly why it had happened. Better than Bill did. In his opinion, Bill had overreacted, and he said as much to his mother when he walked her back to her own room.

"I'm not sure I blame him. The kids hit pretty hard, and he's not used to that. He doesn't have kids, he hasn't been married in a long time. I think his feelings were hurt. He feels like he can't measure up to your father."

"Give him time," Peter smiled. "They'll get used to him," he said hopefully.

"I hope so."

She lay on her bed in the dark for a while, in her brown velvet suit, with her shoes off, thinking about Jack, and Bill, and her children. It was a complicated situation, and she had her own grief and feelings to contend with. There was hardly room for them, she was always too busy dealing with other people. And as she lay there, she started to cry as she thought of her husband and how much she missed him. He had left a huge hole behind, and sometimes it seemed like there was no way to fill it. She loved Bill, but not the way she had loved her husband. At least not yet, but she thought she might someday. It would always be different because they were different people.

The phone rang while she was still lying there in the dark, and she reached out a hand to answer it, without turning the light on. It was Bill, and he sounded stressed. He didn't sound any better than he had when he left. In fact, he sounded slightly worse, but he said there was something he had to tell her.

"What's that?" she asked, with her eyes closed, still missing Jack, and feeling terrible about what had happened. She still felt as though she had Everest to climb, and she had been climbing for eleven months now.

"I'm sorry, Liz. I can't do this. I've thought about it, and I don't know what happened to me. I think I went kind of crazy for a while. I met you and fell in love with you, and your family looks so wholesome from the outside, and you were so vulnerable, I just fell into it like a trap. But it's not me, and I want out now." Her eyes opened brusquely and she stared into the darkness as she listened.

"What are you saying to me?" But she knew. He had already made it clear, she just didn't want to hear it.

"I'm saying that I made a mistake, and it's over. I love you, and your kids are great. But I just can't do it. Megan did us all a big favor today. It could have taken us months or even years to see it this clearly. I had blinding clarity after I left. I went running, and it all came clear to me. I was insane for a while, but now I'm not . . . Liz . . . I'm sorry . . . but it's over." She couldn't even find words to say to him. She lay there feeling as though someone had hit her in the chest and knocked the wind out of her. She was speechless. And all she could think of were the waves of panic that had engulfed her when Jack died. And now she was losing Bill. She had barely had time to get used to him, to let him into her heart, but he was lodged there in spite of it, and now he was prying himself out. It was over. In one fell swoop, she had lost him. Thank you, Megan.

"Don't you want to think about this for a while?" She tried to reason with him, as she would have one of her children. "You're panicking, and your feelings are hurt. They'll get used to you, you know. All they need is time."

"There's no point, Liz. This isn't what I want. I see that clearly now. We should both be grateful." But she wasn't grateful. She was devastated. "I'll call in a few days to see how you are. I'm sorry, I really am, but this is the way it was meant to be. I know it." How did he know? And what did he know? Two of her daughters had been rude to him, but they were just children, and they missed their father.

"Why don't you just calm down, and we'll talk about it later."

"There's nothing to talk about." He sounded panicked.

"I'm out, Liz. I told you, it's over. You have to understand that." Why? Why did she have to understand everyone else's bad behavior? Why did she have to make excuses for him and her children? Why did she have to be the one who lost every time? They had lost too, but she had lost even more than they had.

"I love you," she said clearly, as tears began to choke her.

"You'll get over it. So will I. I don't need another divorce, and you don't need another headache. You have enough without me. Just tell the kids to relax, the moron is out of their lives. They can celebrate now." He sounded bitter and angry and like a petulant child, but she couldn't reach him.

"Jamie loves you, and so does Peter. What am I supposed to tell them?"

"That we made a mistake, and we realized it before it was too late. It'll be a relief to them, and to us too one day. I'm going to hang up now, Liz. There's nothing left to say. Good-bye." He said it with such finality that it took her breath away, and he hung up before she could even answer.

She lay holding the receiver in the dark, and she was crying when she set it down. She couldn't believe what had just happened. Just like that. He'd had "blinding" clarity and it was over. "Blinding" seemed to be the operative word here. And she wanted to shake him. But she wasn't even angry at him, she was just devastated. And this time, when she cried herself to sleep that night, it was for Bill, and not her husband.

Chapter 11

Liz dragged herself through the next few days, after the Thanksgiving fiasco, and she didn't say anything to anyone about Bill walking out on her after Thanksgiving, not even to Victoria when they spoke on the phone, and least of all to her mother, who would have had a lot to say about it. Her mother had told her beforehand that it was a mistake to invite him to Thanksgiving. And Liz had just thought she was jealous, because she hadn't invited her to come out, although they had talked about her coming for Christmas.

But after Thanksgiving, Liz hadn't looked as bad in months. She was sad and tired, and irritable with the children. At first, both Carole and Jean thought it was the agony of the upcoming holidays, and the memories they evoked. But it was Jean who finally understood what had happened. Bill had stopped calling.

"Did you two have a fight?" she asked gingerly, when Liz came back from court the week after Thanksgiving.

Liz looked up at her with a grim expression, and there were dark circles under her eyes. She had lost weight in the past few days, and she was sleeping even less than she had been. "He walked out on me. The kids treated him like shit at Thanksgiving, or at least Megan and Annie did. And it was too much for him. They were incredibly rude actually, but apparently that was all he needed to convince him that it was all a big mistake, and our romance was the result of temporary insanity. Two weeks ago, he asked me to marry him on Valentine's Day. But we never made it through Thanksgiving."

"Maybe he's just panicked," Jean said cautiously. She hadn't seen Liz look that bad in months and it worried her. She seemed desperately unhappy, and it hadn't gone well for her in court that day. She had lost the motion, which just seemed to add to her depression. But the real issue was Bill and not the motion. "He'll be back, Liz. Let him calm down for a few days."

"I don't think so. I think he meant it." And she was sure of it when she called him at the end of the week, and he didn't return her call. And hating herself for it, she paged him. He called her back finally, after a few hours, and said he'd been tied up with an emergency, but his voice was distant and very chilly.

"I just wanted to see if you were okay," she said, trying to sound lighthearted, but he clearly had no interest in pursuing a conversation.

"I'm fine, Liz. Thanks for the call. Look, I'm sorry, but I'm busy."

"Call me sometime." She hated herself for sounding pathetic, but he was as direct as ever with her.

"I don't think that's a good idea right now. We both need to lick our wounds and get over what happened."

"What did happen?" she asked, pressing him, and it was obvious he didn't like it.

"You know what happened. I came to my senses. I don't fit into your family, Liz, and I don't even want to try. You're a great woman and I love you, but this will never work. Not for me at least. You need to find someone else when you and the kids get over losing Jack, and that could take a while." But it wasn't Jack she'd been thinking of for the past week, it was Bill. For the first time in eleven months, Jack seemed to be fading into the distance, and the pain Bill had inflicted on her as he left was far more acute, and more distressing.

"If we really love each other, we can work it out. Why don't we try?"

"For one very good reason," he said bluntly, "I don't want to. I don't want to be married, or have kids, particularly someone else's kids who don't want me. They made it pretty clear, and I got the message."

"They'd adjust in time." She was pleading with him, and wishing that she wouldn't. It was humiliating but she didn't care. She knew now how much she loved him. And it seemed to be too late now. He wouldn't even give her a chance to try and work it out, and fix it.

"Maybe they'd adjust, Liz, but I wouldn't. And what's more, I don't want to. Find yourself another guy." It was a callous thing to say to her, but it delivered the message.

"I love *you*. That's not a generic prescription, Doctor."

"I can't help you out," he said coldly. "And I've got to get back to the ER I've got a five-year-old with a tracheotomy sitting there waiting for me. Merry Christmas, Liz." He was brutal, and she wanted to hate him for it, but didn't. She didn't have the energy to hate him. She felt as though someone had pulled the plug on her on Thanksgiving night, and someone had. He had.

She went home that afternoon, feeling sad and beaten, and it didn't help when Jamie looked up from the Christmas cookies he was making with Carole and asked her where Bill was. It was an interesting question. She didn't know what to say to him. Gone? Finished? Over? He doesn't like us anymore? It was hard to find the right answer for him.

"He's . . . busy, Jamie. He doesn't have time to see us right now."

"Did he die?" Jamie asked with a worried expression. In his mind, people who disappeared like his father were probably dead now.

"No, he didn't. But he doesn't want to see us for a while."

"Is he mad at me?"

"No, sweetheart. He isn't."

"He said he'd fly his kite with me, and he never did. The one he made himself."

"Maybe you should ask Santa for one this year," she said, feeling drained. There wasn't much more she could say to him. Bill Webster had walked out of their life and there was nothing she could do about it. Even begging wouldn't have brought him back, and she knew it. Not pleading or cajoling or reasoning or loving. She had tried everything she could think of that afternoon on the phone, and the one thing that was clear to her now was that he didn't want her. There was no arguing with that. He had a right to make that decision.

"It won't be the same if Santa brings me a kite," Jamie said sadly. "Bill's kite is special because he made it."

"Maybe we can make one," she said, fighting back tears. If she could train him for the running long jump, maybe she could learn how to make a kite. But what else was she supposed to do for them? How much did she have to learn? How many people did she have to be for everyone, because a lunatic had shot Jack, and Bill Webster had decided to walk out on her in a fit of panic? And why did she always have to pick up the pieces? She was haunted by the question.

Carole went to pick the girls up from school shortly afterwards, and as soon as they walked in, Jamie gave them the news his mother had shared with him. "Bill doesn't want to see us anymore."

"Good," Megan said loudly, and then looked faintly guilty as she glanced at her mother. She could see that her mother looked very unhappy.

"That's not a nice thing to say, Meg," Liz said quietly, and she looked so sad that Megan said she was sorry.

"I just don't like him," she added.

"You hardly know him," Liz said and Megan nodded, and the girls went upstairs to do their homework. They only had three more weeks of school before Christmas vacation. But there was no holiday spirit in the house, and it broke Liz's heart when she brought out the decorations.

She decided not to put lights on the outside of the house this year, or in the trees the way Jack always did. They just put up decorations inside the house, and two weeks before Christmas she took them to buy a Christmas tree, but no one's heart was in it.

She hadn't heard from Bill in two weeks by then, and she suspected she never would again. He had made his decision, and intended to stick by it. And she had finally admitted it to Victoria, who was devastated for her, and offered to take her to lunch, but Liz didn't even want to see her.

And as Christmas approached, the entire house seemed to be weighed down, they were all sinking slowly into the mire of depression. It was nearly a year since Jack had died, and it suddenly felt as though it were yesterday. The children talked about him constantly. And Liz felt as though she were ricocheting between her agony over losing Bill and her memories of her late husband. She stayed in her room most of the time, and they didn't entertain friends. She turned down all the invitations to Christmas parties. She even decided not to have her mother come out, and told her she wanted to be alone with her children, and although her mother had sounded hurt, she said she understood it. And she invited another widowed friend to come and stay with her.

The only things Liz and the children did to acknowledge the holiday were hang ornaments on the tree, and bake Christmas cookies, and all she did was pray that the holiday would soon be over.

She thought about taking them to ski between Christmas and New Year's, but they weren't in the mood for that, and they decided to stay home, as they all sank slowly into the quicksand of painful memories that engulfed them.

She was sitting at her desk in the office the week before Christmas when a client called, sounding breathless, and asked if she could come in to see her. Liz had some free time that afternoon, and made an appointment for her. And what she heard when the woman came in didn't please her. The woman's husband was endangering her six-year-old son, he had taken him on the back of his motorcycle on the freeway without a helmet, flew in a helicopter with him, although he'd only just gotten his license, and let him ride his bike to school, in heavy traffic, and again without a helmet. The client wanted Liz to take visitation away from him, and to further make the point, she wanted to go after his business. But as soon as she said it, it had a familiar ring to Liz, and she shook her head firmly.

"We're not going to do that to him," Liz said without a moment's hesitation. "I'll ask for mediation, and we'll get them to work out a list of things that he can't do with your son. But we're not going to take him to court, and we're not going after his business." She said it so vehemently that the client looked at her with suspicion.

"Why not?" For a minute, she thought her husband had gotten to her.

"Because the price is too high," Liz said simply. She had lost ten pounds in the last three weeks, and she looked tired and pale, but she looked so definite and so grim that the woman listened. "I had a case like that once before, not involving a child. But the only way to get the man's attention was by freezing his assets and his business."

"Did it work?" the woman asked hopefully, it sounded good to her, but not to Liz.

"No, it didn't. He killed his wife, himself, and my husband last year on Christmas Day. If you hit your husband too hard, he may hurt you or your son. And I'm not going to be a party to that." There was a long silence between them as the woman nodded.

"I'm sorry."

"Thank you, so am I. Now here's what we are going to do." They made a list of dangerous activities that he wouldn't be allowed to do, and Liz called the court-appointed mediator while the woman sat there. But the mediation office was swamped and the first appointment they could give her was on January eleventh. It was three and a half weeks away, and to help the situation along, Liz agreed to write him a letter of warning in the meantime.

"It won't do anything," the woman looked at Liz bleakly. "If you don't hit him over the head with a hammer, he won't get it."

"If we do, maybe you or your son will," Liz repeated. "And I know you don't want that." It was an impressive threat, and the woman left Liz's office feeling helpless. But at least Liz felt she hadn't jeopardized her client or her son when she went home that night, and the kids finally seemed in better spirits.

It had been the last day of school that day, and Carole had promised to take the four younger ones skating. Peter and his new girlfriend had a date for dinner and a movie. And Liz was looking forward to a quiet evening alone when the phone rang at nine-thirty. The voice on the other end was hysterical, and it took her a minute to recognize it. It was the client she had seen that afternoon, for whom she had scheduled the mediation. And to give her a sense of security, she had given her her home phone number. The woman's name was Helene, and she sounded nearly incoherent.

"Helene, calm down, and try to tell me what happened." It took more than five minutes to understand the story clearly. Her husband, Scott, had taken their son Justin joyriding on the hills in San Francisco on his motorcycle. She wasn't sure if he'd been drunk or not, but it was a possibility, and the child hadn't been wearing a helmet, when they were hit by a truck. Both of Justin's legs were broken, and he had a head injury, although by some miracle he had landed in a patch of grass outside someone's house. He was in pediatric intensive care at Children's Hospital in San Francisco, and his father was in critical condition and still in a coma. The police had come to her house to tell her. The only comforting part of the story for Liz was that even if she'd agreed to take the son of a bitch to court, they wouldn't have gotten there yet, and it wouldn't have changed what had just happened. It wasn't her fault, but whether or not it was, Helene's little boy was in grave danger.

"Where are you now?" Liz asked as she stood up and reached for her handbag still sitting on the end of her bed.

"I'm at the ICU at Children's."

"Is someone with you?"

"No, I'm alone," she sobbed into the phone. She was from New York, and wanted to move back, as soon as her husband would agree to let her.

"I'll be there in twenty minutes," Liz said, and hung up on her without waiting for an answer. She grabbed her coat on her way out the front door, glad that she had decided not to go skating with her children. She'd been feeling guilty about it, but she'd been so tired and depressed that she had opted not to.

She parked her car outside the hospital eighteen minutes later, and when she got to the ICU, she found Helene sobbing in the arms of a nurse. They had just taken Justin upstairs to put pins in both his legs, but the nurse said he was conscious and the head injury was nothing more than a bad concussion. The child, and his mother, had been very lucky. But sitting in the hospital with her, as they waited, reminded her of Bill again. She wondered how he was, and what he was doing. She knew there was no point thinking about it anymore, it had been more than three weeks now, and she knew he wasn't going to call her. He had made up his mind, and stuck to it. Bill was that kind of person. And the terrors she and her family represented were just too much for him.

Justin came back from the operating room shortly after midnight. He was still sedated, and his legs were bandaged to the hip and he looked like a little rag doll as he lay there, but the doctor said he'd be as good as new eventually, and in six months or a year, they'd take the pins out.

Helene cried as she listened to him, but she was calmer than she'd been when Liz had arrived. They had talked for hours about what they were going to do. She had finally convinced Liz. They were going to court, and putting every restriction on her husband they could, and then Liz wanted her to go back to New York. Helene was young and had family there, and even an old boyfriend who'd been calling and was hinting about marriage. Liz wanted her out of town and as far from her ex-husband as she could get her.

"And then," she looked at Helene with a sad smile, as the child's mother walked her to the elevator and thanked her for keeping her company all night. "And then, I'm going to retire," Liz said, with a sigh of relief. It was all she wanted. She'd had it with family law, and she'd been thinking about it for months. This was all she'd needed to convince her. She'd thought about it again on the way to the hospital and she was sure now.

"What are you going to do instead?"

"Grow roses," she laughed, "and clip coupons. No, actually, I'm going to do something I really want to do, and have for a long time. I'm going to be an advocate for children. I'm going to work out of my house, and close the office I shared with my husband. I've done it alone for the last year, and it just isn't what I want." She looked better than she had in weeks when she said it, and Helene thanked Liz again before she left.

"I'll call you when I get a court date." She smiled at her client as the elevator doors closed, and she knew as she walked to her car with a lighter step that she had made the right decision. She wondered if that was how Bill had felt when he called to tell her it was over. Maybe it was, she thought to herself. Maybe she had been as big a burden for him, and as wrong, as the practice she had shared with Jack had become for her once he was gone. If so, she had to respect Bill's decision. But she had made hers that night, finally, as she sat holding Helene's hand, wanting to kill her ex-husband for what he had done to Justin, out of pure wanton negligence and irresponsibility. Helene's ex-husband was still in a coma when Liz left the hospital, and there was a possibility of brain damage, but at least Justin was going to be all right, and to Liz, that was all that mattered.

She drove into her driveway on Hope Street shortly after one o'clock, and everyone was in bed, except Peter, who had just come in from his date, and he was surprised to see his mother. She never went anywhere anymore, except court and work. He hadn't seen her out in the evening since Bill left.

"Where were you, Mom?"

"At the hospital, with a client. It's a long story." They chatted for a minute and then she went up to bed. She was absolutely exhausted, but pleased with the decision she'd made that night. She knew without a doubt it was the right one.

And the next morning when she got to the office, she called the court and set a date for a hearing. She called Helene at the hospital to tell her. Helene said Justin was all right, and he'd be going home with her in a few days, but when Liz told her about the court date, she said quietly that they didn't need one.

"You're not feeling guilty about going to court against him, are you, Helene? No judge in any county would be sympathetic to a man who took his six-year-old son out on a motorcycle without a helmet. You've got the goods on him now, you might as well use them."

"I don't need to."

"Why not?" Liz looked blank as she waited. Her mind was already full of what she was going to say at the hearing. It was set for the week between Christmas and New Year's.

"Scott died of a massive brain hemorrhage last night," she said quietly, and to her credit, she sounded sad. But he had been her husband, and her son's father.

"Oh . . ." Liz said, startled into silence for a moment. "I'm sorry."

"So am I . . . I've hated him for the past two years, but he's still Justin's father. I haven't told him yet." Hearing that made Liz squeeze her eyes shut, and it brought home to her what had happened.

"I'm really sorry." The child was going to be heartbroken, even if Helene wasn't. "Let me know if there's anything I can do to help you."

"I guess you know what that's like, for your kids, I mean."

"Yes, I do. It's going to be hard for a long time. We haven't gotten over it yet."

"I'm going back to New York to stay with my parents, as soon as Justin can travel."

"That sounds like a good idea."

They hung up a minute later, and Liz was still looking pensive when Jean wandered into her office. "What was that all about?" She had heard Liz telling Helene she was sorry, and knew she'd been with her at the hospital nearly all night. She looked shocked when Liz told her.

"It's incredible the things people are willing

to do to their kids,'' Jean said, with a look of disapproval.

"Which brings me to another piece of bad news," Liz said, feeling guilty, but she had wanted to tell her all morning. It was good news for her, but not for Jean. And Liz was going to be sorry to lose her. "I don't know how to tell you this, except straight on," which was how Liz did everything, it was one of the things Jean loved about her. "I'm closing the office."

"You're retiring?" Jean looked stunned, although she knew she shouldn't have. Liz had been carrying an insanely heavy load ever since her husband died, and Jean had figured that it was only a matter of time before Liz decided she just couldn't do it. The truth was she could, but she didn't want to. Not without Jack. And she didn't want another partner.

"I'm going to work part-time, from home, on child advocacy. It's what I really loved about what we did. I hated all the catfights and all the fancy footwork, and all the bravado and bullshit. That was always more Jack's style than mine. I care about the kids, and that's all I want to do now."

Jean smiled generously at her, and came around the desk to give her a hug. "You did the right thing, kid. This place is going to kill you. You'll be great at the child advocacy stuff."

"I hope so." Liz looked worried then. "But what are you going to do? I've been thinking about it all morning."

"It's time for me to grow up too. This may sound crazy at my age"—she was forty-three—"I want to go to law school." Liz beamed at her, and then laughed. It was the perfect solution.

"Well, don't go into family law, you'll hate it."

"I want to go into criminal, and work in the prosecutor's office."

"Good for you." Liz estimated it would take her three months to wind up all her cases, and then she wanted to take a few months off, and let everyone know what she'd be doing. She had earned a break, and she wanted to spend the time with her children. They had been patient for the last year, while she kept a dozen balls in the air, and worked long hours and endless days. She felt as though she owed it to them to take a break now.

"If I apply to law school before the end of the year," Jean said, looking pleased, "I should be able to start in June, or at the latest September. That'll give me a couple of months off too. It'll do us both good." They both felt as though they had aged a century in the last year, although they didn't look it.

Liz was still sitting at her desk chatting with

Jean when Carole called, and Jean thought she detected a note of panic, but Jean didn't say anything to Liz when she told her Carole was on the phone. She figured it was just her imagination, and Carole was too busy over Christmas with the kids home.

"Hi there." Liz was feeling expansive and relaxed, after having made her momentous decision. "What's up?"

"Jamie." The way she said it rang a bell from the previous summer. She was speaking in shorthand.

"What happened?" Liz felt a sudden wave of panic as she waited for an answer.

"He was trying to hang a papier-mâché angel we made on the Christmas tree. He got the ladder out while I was doing something for Meg, and he fell. I think his arm is broken."

"Shit." It was five days before Christmas. And now that Liz listened carefully, she could hear him crying in the background.

"How bad is it?"

"It's at a very nasty angle."

"I'll meet you at the hospital as soon as I can get there." At least it was nothing as dramatic as what had happened to Peter, or little Justin the night before. But it was the first time Jamie had broken anything, and she knew he'd be panicked. She grabbed her coat and bag and ran out the door as Jean asked her what had happened. "Broken arm," Liz shouted as she ran down the stairs. There never seemed to be a minute to just sit down and enjoy life. But what was there to enjoy these days anyway? Christmas was looming like a boulder about to fall on them, Jack was gone, and so was Bill now too. Merry Christmas.

Chapter 12

Liz flew into the hospital emergency room as she had the night before at Children's for Helene, and this time she was the anxious mother and not the professional comforter. It was a little different. Jamie was obviously in pain when she arrived, and screamed every time one of the nurses tried to touch him, and it made Liz feel sick when she looked at the way his arm was sticking out. There was no doubt about the fact that it was broken. The only question was how badly.

They were trying to reason with him when she arrived, but they had already concluded that they were going to have to sedate him, and they were going to take him up to surgery to set the arm.

An orthopedic surgeon had been called, and Carole looked guilty and frantic.

"I'm so sorry, Liz . . . I took my eyes off him for five minutes. . . ."

"It's all right, it could have happened if I was home too." Jamie did things like that sometimes. All kids did. And Jamie was a little less sensible and less steady than most boys his age, for obvious reasons. Liz tried fruitlessly to calm him down, but he was screaming so loud he couldn't even hear her. He was in so much pain, he just sat on the gurney shrinking from all of them, and wouldn't let her hold him. It was very upsetting. And she was looking frazzled and worn out as she tried to talk to him again, and heard a familiar voice just behind her shoulder. "What's going on here?"

Liz turned instinctively and found herself looking into the eyes of Bill Webster. He had been in the ER to take a patient to the trauma unit when he heard the fuss, and saw the familiar red hair, and couldn't stop himself from coming over. "What happened?" he asked her, without introduction or greeting.

"He fell off a ladder and broke his arm," she said simply, as he walked in front of Jamie and put himself in the child's field of vision to be sure he saw him. And for an instant, the wailing abated. It tuned down to vehement sobs, and as

Jamie looked at Bill, his little shoulders were heaving.

"What happened, champ? Were you training for the Olympics again? It's not time yet. Didn't you know that?" He gently reached for the arm, and although Jamie shrank from him, he didn't scream or jump off the gurney, and let Bill touch him.

"I fffelllll . . . offffff . . . a lllladddder."

"Putting something on the Christmas tree?" Jamie nodded. "You know what we're going to do? We're going to give you a cast for that arm, and you have to make me a promise. Will you do that?"

"Wwwwhhhatt's the ppppromise?" Jamie was shaking from head to foot from all the crying, but as Bill talked to him he was gently feeling the arm, and distracting Jamie. And the child made no objection, as his mother watched him.

"I want to be the first one to sign your cast. Is that a deal? Not the second or the third . . . I've got to be first. Okay?"

"Okay," Jamie nodded, as the surgeon arrived, and the two doctors conferred, and as they finished, Bill glanced at Liz. She was looking very thin, and at the moment distraught over Jamie's broken arm, which was why he had made the suggestion he just had to the surgeon.

"You know what we're going to do?" Bill

asked Jamie as though he had a terrific surprise for him. "We're going to go upstairs and put on your cast now. And I'm going to come with you, just to be sure that no one else signs it first. How does that sound to you? You're going to sleep for a few minutes, and when you wake up, presto magic, the cast will be on, and I'll sign it."

"Can I make the bed go up and down?" He still remembered that from Peter's stay there.

"We'll find you one you can turn every way you want, but first let's get that cast on." He glanced at Liz to reassure her, and she nodded. She knew then what he had done, he had asked the surgeon if he could stay in the OR with Jamie, and the gesture touched her. She wanted to thank him, but he was already pushing Jamie toward the elevator on the gurney, and the surgeon was right behind them. She didn't want to call out to the child for fear that it would remind him that she couldn't go with him. So instead she huddled in a chair miserably, worrying about him, and thinking about Bill. It had been a shock to see him, but there had been so much else happening that they couldn't even speak to each other, which was probably better. There was nothing left to say anyway. It had been a month since she'd seen him, and it felt like aeons. She still cried herself to sleep at night over him, but there was no way for him to know that.

It was over an hour before they returned, and when they did, Jamie was still groggy, and Bill was still with him. The surgeon had gone on to another case, and Bill told her very professionally that everything had gone smoothly. It had been a clean break, and in six weeks they could take the cast off. They'd even given him one he could wear in the shower.

"He should wake up in a few minutes. He did fine upstairs. We put him out so fast he never knew what hit him." She couldn't help but remember how gruff he'd been with her the first time they met, and notice how gentle he was with Jamie now. He was a man of a million facets. And Megan calling him a "brute" made her wince even more than before. It had been inexcusable, and she knew it. "Do you want a cup of coffee while he wakes up? It might be a little while, maybe twenty minutes."

"Do you have time?" She didn't want to impose on him. She knew how busy he was, and he had already spent nearly two hours with Jamie.

"I have time," he said, leading her down the hall to a room where the ER doctors relaxed between cases. But there was no one in the room when they got there. And he handed her a steaming cup of coffee. "He'll be fine, Liz, don't worry about him."

"Thanks for being so nice to him. I appreciate it a lot. He was scared to death when I got here."

Bill smiled as he nodded and poured himself a cup of coffee. "He damn near screamed the house down. I wondered what was happening, that's why I came over. Great set of lungs on Master Jamie." She smiled, and their eyes met. But neither of them acknowledged more than Jamie's broken arm. And it was obvious that they felt awkward with each other. He looked as though he had lost weight too, and he seemed pale and tired, but Christmas was busy for him. There were lots of drunk drivers and broken hips and traumas she couldn't even dream of, like what had happened to Justin, and now Jamie. Though Bill usually only handled the major disasters, like Peter's accident. "You look well," he said finally, and she nodded, not sure what to respond to him. She could hardly tell him that she thought of him night and day and had figured out how much she loved him. It was a little late for that.

"You must be busy over the holidays," she said to make idle conversation. Everything else she could have said sounded either argumentative or pathetic. And there was no point trying to sell him something he knew he didn't want. If he had wanted it, or changed his mind, he would have called. His silence was the final message. And she heard it loud and clear.

"I am pretty busy. How's Peter?" He was keeping the conversation to neutral topics, like his patient.

"As good as new," she smiled, "and madly in love."

"Good for him. Tell him I said hi." With that, he looked at his watch and suggested they go back to Jamie. "He should be wide awake now." He was, and he was asking for Bill and his mother, and he smiled when he saw them. "You didn't forget your promise, did you, champ?" Jamie shook his head with a broad grin, and Bill whipped a marker out of his pocket. He wrote a little poem to him, and drew a little dog, and then signed it, and Jamie was ecstatic.

"You were first, Bill, I promised!"

"You sure did." Bill smiled at him, and then hugged him, as Liz watched them, feeling her heart ache. This was what she had lost when he walked out of her life on Thanksgiving. But she already knew exactly what she had lost, and there was nothing she could do about it. He had made up his mind.

"You never flew your kite with me," Jamie said, as he looked at him, and Bill looked a little startled, and then dismayed.

"You're right, I didn't. I'll call your mom someday, and we'll take it out for a spin. Maybe after you get your cast off. How does that sound?"

"Good." He nodded, satisfied, and Bill lifted him off the gurney, and set him gently on his feet.

"Now, will you stay off that ladder for me?" Jamie nodded, his eyes filled with admiration. Bill was his hero. "And don't climb the Christmas tree either."

"Mom won't let me."

"I'm glad to hear it. Now, say hi to Peter and your sisters for me. I'll see you soon, Jamie. Merry Christmas."

"My daddy died on Christmas," Jamie informed him, and Liz felt her heart flinch. It was a reminder none of them needed.

"I know," Bill said respectfully. "I'm sorry, Jamie."

"Me too. It was a very bad Christmas."

"I'm sure it was, for your whole family. I hope this one will be better."

"I asked Santa for a kite like yours, but Mom says he won't bring one. She says we have to buy one."

"Or make one," Bill corrected. "What else did you ask Santa for?"

"A puppy, but Mom says we won't get that either, because Carole is allergic. She has asthma. I asked for games too, and a Nerf gun."

"I'll bet you get those for sure." Jamie nodded, and thanked him for the cast and for signing it, and then Bill turned his eyes to the child's mother. He could feel her watching them and there was something so sad in her eyes that it burned right through him. "I hope Christmas will be okay for all of you. I know the first year won't be easy."

"It's got to be better than last year," she smiled, with her mouth, if not her eyes, and he wanted to push back a lock of hair that had fallen across her eyes, but he didn't think he should. She did it herself a minute later, unaware that he had seen it. "Thank you for being so good to Jamie. I appreciate it."

"That's what I do. Brute that I am," he grinned at her, and she looked embarrassed. "I got over it," he said to put her at ease again, "though I'll admit it smarted for a bit. Girls play dirty," he said and laughed as he walked them to the door of the ER.

"Not all girls," she said softly. "Take care, Bill. Merry Christmas." She waved as she and Jamie left. Carole had gone home to the others while Jamie was in surgery. And Bill stood watching them as they got in the car, and then walked back through the emergency room with his hands in his pockets and his head down.

Chapter 13

When Jamie got home from the hospital, he told everyone he'd seen Bill, and told Peter he'd said hi to him, and then he showed them his cast and where Bill had signed it. He had everyone sign it then, including Carole and his mother. Liz watched him, feeling as though she'd been trapped in a whirlpool all afternoon, with her own emotions whirling all around her. It had been hard seeing Bill, but it was nice too. It was so tantalizing, she had wanted to just reach out and touch him. Or worse yet, tell him she loved him. But she knew that that would have been crazy. He was as far out of her life now as Jack was.

She went to the cemetery to leave flowers for her husband the next day. And she stood there

284

for a long time, thinking of the years they had shared, and the good times they'd had. It all seemed so wasted now, so lost, all because of one terrible moment. It still seemed so unfair. She stood at his grave for a long time, and cried for what they had lost and what he was missing. He would never see his children grow up, or his grandchildren, he wouldn't grow old with her. Everything had stopped, and now they had to go on without him. It was all so very hard.

But the worst agony of all was Christmas Eve and Christmas Day. Although she had expected it to be difficult, she had been in no way prepared for how hard it would hit her. It was like a wrecking ball to the chest that hit her in all ways. She missed the joys they had shared, the Christmases when the children were small, the laughter, the promise, the traditions. And then, as she reeled from the blow of her memories, she remembered the horror of their last Christmas morning, watching him lie dying on their office floor with no way to stop the nightmare that befell them. She walked around in a fog all day, crying all the time, and unable to stop, and the children were no better. It was one of the worst days in her life since he had died. And her mother was worried about her when she called. And even more so when she told her she was closing the office.

"I knew you'd have to do that," her mother

said the minute she told her. "Did you lose all your clients?" Nothing had changed in the past year since her dire predictions after the funeral.

"No, Mom, I have too many. I can't keep it up anymore, and I'm tired of it. I don't want to do family law. I'm going to represent children."

"And who's going to pay?"

Liz smiled at the question. "The court, or their parents, or the agencies that hire me. Don't worry. I know what I'm doing." Her mother spoke to all the children and told Liz they sounded depressed, which was no wonder. It was a rough Christmas for them all.

And her friend Victoria called her from Aspen. She surprised Liz by saying she had decided to go back into practice part-time, and she made Liz promise that in spite of that, they were going to see more of each other and Liz promised that they would. Victoria was worried about her and the children. She knew it was a brutal Christmas for them, and she was sorry she wasn't there to come over and visit.

But for the rest of the day, the phone was silent. And at the end of the day, Liz took them all to a movie. They were as sad as she was, and they needed some distraction. They went to see a comedy, and the kids laughed, but Liz didn't. She felt as though there were nothing left in her life to laugh at. It was all tragedy and loss, and people who had died or walked away. She soaked in a hot bath after they got home, and just lay there for a long time, thinking of how fast the year had gone and how much had been in it, and in spite of herself, she couldn't help wondering where Bill was. He was probably working. He had always said he hated holidays, that they were for people with families, and he had opted not to have one, after his taste of it at Thanksgiving, although she wasn't entirely sure she blamed him. But she thought he could at least have given it another chance. If he'd been brave enough, which he wasn't. She knew she had to face the fact now that he just didn't want it. He liked the life he had, and he was good at it. She lay in the tub thinking of how kind he'd been to Jamie. He was a terrific doctor, and a decent man.

She went to bed alone that night, just after midnight. Jamie was sleeping in his own room. He had slept in hers once since he got the cast, turned over in the middle of the night, and accidentally hit her with it, and she still had a bruise on her shoulder to show for it. After that, they'd agreed that it would be better if he slept in his own bed till he got the cast off.

"You okay, Mom?" Peter stuck his head in her room when he came upstairs right after she went to bed, and she told him she was, and thanked him for checking. They had stayed close to each other all day, like survivors in the water, clinging to a single life raft. It had been a Christmas they would always remember, not as bad as the last one, but nearly as painful in its own way. All she wanted to do now was go to sleep, and wake up when the holidays were over. But as usual now, sleep eluded her for hours, and she lay in bed, awake, thinking of Jack, and Bill, and her children. And finally, shortly after four o'clock, she drifted off, and thought she was dreaming when she heard the phone ring. She was in such a dead sleep as she reached out for it, that it took her a while to find it, but no one else in the house answered either.

"Hello?" Her voice was muffled by the sheets, and she sounded groggy, and the person who had called her hesitated for a long moment. She was about to hang up when he finally spoke. She didn't recognize the voice at first, and then she knew it. It was Bill, and she had no idea why he had called. He was probably working. It was still dark outside and she squinted at the clock. It was six-thirty in the morning.

"Hi there," he sounded painfully cheerful, and she felt like a rodeo rider who had been bucked from here to Kentucky after the agonies of the day before. She was exhausted. "I thought I'd call and wish you Merry Christmas."

"Merry Christmas. Wasn't that yesterday?" Or

was she in the Twilight Zone and it was never-ending. A lifetime of Christmases every day forever. It would have been her worst nightmare.

"Yeah. I must have missed it. I was pretty busy. How's Jamie?"

"Fine, I think. Asleep." She stretched, and made an effort to wake up, wondering why he had called her. He seemed pretty chatty for six-thirty in the morning. "You were very nice to him when he broke his arm. Thank you."

"He's a nice kid, and I like him." There was a long silence then, and she started dozing, and then woke with a start, wondering if she'd said something stupid. But she hadn't missed much. Bill seemed to be thinking. Then he asked her, "How was Christmas?" But he could imagine it. He had thought about her all day, and worried about her and the children, which was why he had finally called. That, and a number of other reasons, some of them clearer than others.

"Worse than I expected," she said honestly. "Like having open-heart surgery without an anesthetic."

"I'm sorry, Liz. I thought it might be like that. At least it's over."

"Till next year," she said, sounding grim. She was awake now, and the memory of the day before still made her wince.

"Maybe next year will be better."

"I'm not in any hurry to find out. It'll take me all year to get over this one. How about you? What did you do?"

"I was working."

"I thought so. You must have been busy."

"Very. But I thought about you a lot."

She hesitated and then nodded, lying in the dark, thinking about him. "I thought about you too. I'm sorry things got so messed up. I don't know, I guess I wasn't ready, and the kids were awful."

"And I panicked," he admitted. "I didn't handle it very maturely."

"I'm not sure I would have either," she said graciously, but she would have come back to try and fix it, and he hadn't. But she didn't say that to him.

"I've missed you." He sounded wistful. It had hit him hard when he saw her when Jamie broke his arm, and she had haunted him ever since, until he called.

"So have I. It's been a long month," she said softly.

"Too long," he admitted. "We should have lunch sometime."

"I'd like that." She wondered if he'd ever do it. Maybe he was just lonely and tired, or a patient had died, or Christmas had gotten to him. She didn't have the feeling he wanted to come back, just to touch her, and drift away again. In the end, she had decided, he was a loner, and happier that way.

"How about lunch today?" She was startled when he asked her.

"Today? Sure, I . . ." And then she remembered. "I promised to take the kids skating. How about coffee afterwards?"

"I was really thinking about lunch." He sounded disappointed.

"What about tomorrow?"

"I'm working," he said firmly. She smiled as she realized they were negotiating dates at six-forty-five in the morning. "What about now?" He sounded matter-of-fact as he asked.

"Now? You mean now, as in this minute?"

"Sure, I happen to have a bag lunch in my car, we could share it."

"Where are you?" She was beginning to wonder if he was drunk. He sounded a little crazy to her.

"Actually," he answered nonchalantly, "I'm in your driveway." She got out of bed, as he said it, with the phone in her hand, and peeked out the window. His old Mercedes was sitting in her driveway with the lights off.

"What are you doing out there?" She was watching him, as she said it, and he glanced up and waved at her, as she giggled. "This is crazy."

"I just thought I'd drop by and see if you wanted to have lunch or something. I didn't know if you were busy, or . . . well, you know, since I was such a jerk for the last month, I wasn't sure if I'd have to hang around to convince you. Liz," his voice sounded emotional, as she stood at the window and looked down on him in his car, and he looked up at her, holding his car phone. "I love you." She could see him say it.

"I love you too," she said softly. "Why don't you come in?"

"I'll bring lunch."

"Just bring you. I'll see you in a minute, don't ring the doorbell." She hung up, and ran downstairs to open the door for him, and she saw him get out of his car and wrestle something large and cumbersome out of the backseat, and it took him a minute. And then as he came toward her, carrying it, she saw what it was. It was the kite he had made, and he brought it inside with him. "What are you doing with that?" The whole thing was utterly absurd. His call, his lunch invitation, his visit, his kite. But she loved him, and she knew it, as she looked at him. She had known it for months, she just hadn't been ready before.

"It's for Jamie," he said simply, setting the kite down in her hallway, and then he stood looking down at her, with everything he felt for her in his eyes. He didn't even have to say it. "I love you,

Liz. And Megan was right. I was a moron and a brute. I should have come back the next day, but I was too scared."

"So was I. But I think I figured it out faster than you did. It's been a hell of a long month without you."

"I had to figure out how much I missed you, but I'm back now. If you'll have me."

"I'll have you," she whispered, and then looked worried. "What about the kids, can you stand them?"

"Some easier than others. I'll get used to the rest, and if Megan gives me a hard time, I'll put a cast over her mouth. That should do it." Liz laughed as he pulled her into his arms and kissed her. And they both jumped when they heard a loud voice just behind her.

"What's THAT?" It was Jamie, and he was pointing at the kite Bill had brought with him.

"It's your kite. I figured you had more time to use it than I do. I'll show you how to fly it."

"Oh, boy!" He jumped right into Bill's arms, and nearly knocked his mother over. "Wow! Can I really have it!"

"You sure can."

And then Jamie looked at him suspiciously. "What are you doing here? I thought you were mad at Mom, and Megan."

"I was, but I'm better now."

"Were you mad at me too?" Jamie asked with interest, holding the kite by the frame. He looked like a Norman Rockwell painting.

"Never. I was never mad at you. And I'm not mad at anyone now."

"Good. Can we have breakfast?" Jamie asked his mother.

"In a minute." And as she said it, there were voices from upstairs and Megan shouted down.

"Who's down there?"

"I am," Liz answered. "And Bill and Jamie."

"Bill the doctor?" She sounded surprised, and Liz could hear other voices, Peter and Rachel and Annie. They had woken the whole house up.

"Bill, the Brute and Moron," he corrected, and Megan came down the stairs slowly with a sheepish smile.

"I'm sorry." She looked straight at Bill as she said it.

"Me too." He smiled at her.

"Let's have breakfast," Jamie said again.

"I'll make waffles," Liz said and stopped to look up at Bill, as they exchanged a smile, and he kissed her again.

"You run a busy house," he commented, as he followed her into the kitchen.

"Only sometimes. Come by for lunch anytime," she said, taking out her waffle pan.

"I was thinking of staying," Bill whispered to her.

"I like that idea," she said softly, turning to him.

"So do I," he said, as he picked Jamie up and put him on his shoulders. "I like it a lot in fact." And with that, he turned slowly toward the doorway and saw Megan smiling at him.

DANIELLE STEEL